A PALIMAR SAGA NOVELLA

THE SMUGGLER'S DEAL

A COMPANION TO REMNANT

K. R. SOLBERG | C. R. JACOBSON

EPIC NORTH PUBLISHING

2024 Epic North Publishing

Published in the United States by Epic North Publishing, LLC.

Paperback ISBN 979-8-9863498-3-1
Ebook ISBN 979-8-9863498-4-8
Hercover ISBN 979-8-9863498-5-5

epicnorthpublishing.com

Book design by K. R. Solberg

Cover art by Kaia Bakken

*To the creative writing teachers who cheered us on in our youth,
Mr. Strandquist and Miss. Gustafson.*

And to Lewis, Shane zem'Arta's biggest fan.

CONTENTS

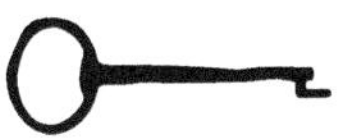

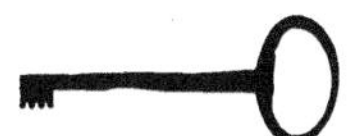

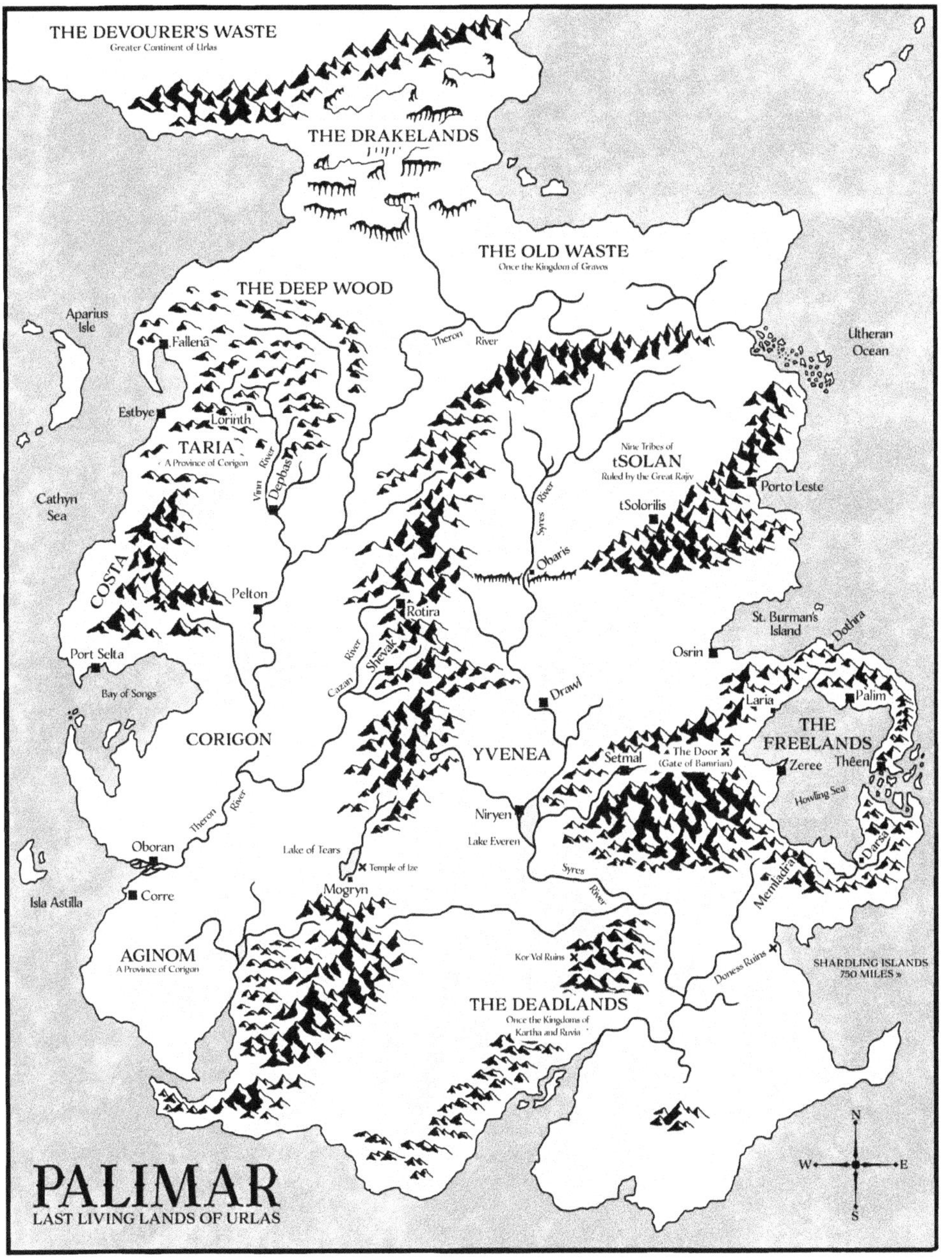
THE DEVOURER'S WASTE
Greater Continent of Urlas
THE DRAKELANDS
THE OLD WASTE
Once the Kingdom of Gravos
THE DEEP WOOD
Aparius Isle
Fallenâ
Estbye
Lorinth
TARIA
A Province of Corigon
Vinn River
Depbas
Theron River
Utheran Ocean
Nine Tribes of
tSOLAN
Ruled by the Great Rajiv
Porto Leste
tSolorilis
Syres River
Obaris
Cathyn Sea
COSTA
Pelton
Rotira
Shevak
Cazan River
St. Burman's Island
Osrin
Dothra
Port Selta
Bay of Songs
Drawl
Laria
Palim
THE FREELANDS
CORIGON
YVENEA
Setmal
The Door
(Gate of Bamrian)
Zeree
Thêen
Howling Sea
Theron River
Niryen
Lake Everen
Oboran
Lake of Tears
Temple of Ize
Syres River
Darsa
Memiadra
Isla Astilla
Corre
Mogryn
AGINOM
A Province of Corigon
Kor Vol Ruins
Doness Ruins
SHARDLING ISLANDS
750 MILES »
THE DEADLANDS
Once the Kingdoms of
Kartha and Ruvia
N
W
E
S
PALIMAR
LAST LIVING LANDS OF URLAS

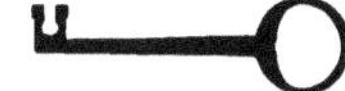

○— 1 —○

AT THE INN

Corre, Agenom
April 14, 1190 PT (Post Tyrannus)

Shane

This hunt had dragged on far too long. Shane zem'Arta surveyed the neighborhood as a temperate evening breeze wafted through the alley. The acrid mixture of sea water and refuse formed a pungent perfume. He winced at the smell. Kneeling beside a splintered crate, he scanned windows broken from the turmoil the city of Corre had suffered lately. Despite heaps of debris, the borough evidenced a previous decadence in its ornate streetlamps and carved details of the buildings. Violent uprisings, sparking like flint on steel, had disappeared quickly, leaving pillars of smoke and social chaos in their wake.

Shane rubbed his eyes and yawned. During the previous night, he and his companions had vacated their inn after a gang of rebels set fire to an adjacent police station.

He already hated being in Drawlen territories. Nothing good happened outside the Freelands. Blinking away his fatigue, he huffed.

"See anything?" Carris asked, crouching behind him. His companion faced the alleyway opening. Her brown bandana hid her pointed goblin ears, and her loose coat concealed several knives. Aginom, a human country, didn't receive sharptooth sapiens warmly.

"No. Just tired," Shane said. "I can't believe that pile of ash managed to get all the way out here. Burning fires."

"Hell of a way to start the year." She punched his arm lightly. "We'll manage. We'll get that little grifter."

"Liiesh will have me fully marked if we don't." He stroked his face, his fingers gliding over the ridges of the two horizontal scars on his left cheek. Another marred his right. In the Freelands, they labeled him a convict, one mark away from being tagged for death. Here in the west, they proved a passing curiosity. Shane licked his sharp teeth and spat on the ground.

Carris scratched her head of spiky black hair using her extended claws. Flexing her fingers, she retracted them. "Liiesh wants this fool brought in alive? How the hell we getting him across fifteen hundred miles of Drawlen territory? Not to mention the burning border."

"I have an idea about that." Shane tapped his forehead.

"A good one? Or will this be Dothra all over again?"

He shrugged. "Dothra wasn't that bad."

She punched him again, causing him to flinch. "My husband nearly broke both his burning legs."

Shane recoiled, massaging his bicep. "He was fine."

Carris rolled her eyes, her vertical pupils pulsing. They scanned the inn across the street, resuming their duty as impatient sentries. Framing the windows, the bright yellow shutters accentuated the vibrance of the blue building. Even in the dimness of oncoming night, the inn stood out among the tar-painted tenements to either side.

The Drawls had made bare wood illegal, part of their tactic to keep the Corigish commonwealth under their crushing grip. This inn must have imported paint from Yvenea, which would have been expensive. And he knew his target liked expensive things. Daeven Kritcher's trail of luxuries had led Shane and part of his crew across the peninsula of Palimar. Shane licked his teeth again.

Carris jumped up, standing shy of five feet, and growled. "He's here."

Shane's eyes locked on the second-floor window at the corner of the inn. A dim, orange light flickered inside.

After a long moment, a stout form silhouetted the panes, shutting the curtains. A black cavity replaced the light of the sun-crystal lamps.

"Was that him?" he asked. "I couldn't get a good look."

"Your eyes getting old, boy?" she barked under her breath. "What are you, twenty?"

He rolled his eyes. "Keep talking, old lady."

She huffed. "Likely his bodyguard. But I can smell his perfume from here."

Shane sniffed. The city's reeking aroma filled his nostrils, along with the faint whiff of musk and honeydew. "Burn me. You've got a nose, Carris."

The goblin woman glanced over her shoulder, grinning. "We gonna say hello?"

He returned his own fanged smile. "We'll even buy him a drink if he comes nicely."

They moved in unison, silent and sinister. The night pressed in, a salty gust cooling Shane's face. After over a month of tracking, he felt the sharp pressure of blood pulse in his ears. There would be retribution for failure in this job.

He slipped into the alley across the street, next to the blue-painted inn. On the ground floor, a door of peeling black tar paint lay ahead of him. He sped up.

"Hold," Carris muttered, grabbing his collar.

He shrugged out of her grip and grunted. Her insistence to operate on an abundance of caution until it came time to rip throats really grated on him. He stepped forward.

Snapping wire twanged, slapping against his boot.

"You rookie whelp," Carris growled.

Simultaneous with Shane's cursing, a bell rang above him, followed by a rumbling of footfalls. Two hulking men, dull-eyed humans, hurtled through the door into the alley.

Shane hunched, extending his claws, and baring his teeth. If these fools had any sense, they would run like cowards rather than tangle with a troll and a goblin in close quarters.

One man whipped a knife from his pocket and offered Shane an ugly smile. "Come at me, ogre."

Carris chuckled, putting up her fist and reciting part of the Karthan war blessing. "May you send a thousand souls to Sovereign's judgement today, warrior."

Shane bumped his fist against hers. "And may your claws never dull." He hurtled toward the knife-wielding thug.

Carris, only reaching Shane's chest at her full height, leapt past him like a hound and rolled under the legs of the other man.

Avoiding the thrust of his opponent's knife, Shane sidestepped and caught the man's head in his iron grip. A brief cry erupted from the man, his skin pale against Shane's dusky hands. Shane slammed his opponent's face against the wall. The man groaned as he slumped onto the gravel and lay still.

Carris forced the other man to his knees, her tarnished flintlock pistol pressed to the back of his neck. In the shadow of the alley, her green eyes glowed, causing the man to recoil.

"P-please," he stammered. "The man said there be gangsters after him. He dun say nothing about no Freelanders. I dun get paid enough for this. Please, lady elf."

Shane hissed at the slur, though the man's tone indicated he meant no insult.

Carris pressed the muzzle of her gun tighter into the man's flesh. "Using that word's a fast way to meet a round shot, boy."

"Sorry!" the man barked. "Goblin . . . I mean kobold, whatever."

Carris chuckled, then holstered her pistol and jutted her chin to the mouth of the alley. "Get you gone."

The man muttered incoherently and scrambled out to the street.

Shane stepped over the other man, who bled from the forehead and groaned. Pressing his boot against the man's side, Shane said, "Follow your friend or meet your maker."

The thug quivered and crawled toward the street as Shane and Carris stepped through the open kitchen door.

The night being young, the space buzzed with activity. The fragrance of stale beer permeated the air. The staff scowled at the pair of them. A portly man stirred steaming broth in the cookpot suspended over a bed of heat stones in the hearth. The sulfuric fragrance of furnace-grade sunrock burned Shane's nostrils. He wrinkled his nose.

Three women cut vegetables at a prep table, black paint chips flying as they chopped.

Shane cringed when he saw the braided indenture collars encircling their necks. In his memory rang the moans for mercy he'd heard so often from the slaver's brig of the *Reaver*. The older woman cursed in Aginomian, waving her chef's knife. Shane caught a few words, mostly insults about being a sharptooth.

A growled order from the man at the hearth silenced her. He set his ladle aside and waddled toward Shane. His golden skin and bound black hair marked him the only native Aginomian in the room.

"I'm a businessman, sharptooth," the man said. "I don't know what you have against dat rich fool, but he's been not'ing but a burning headache since he came. You got a legal warrant?"

Shane let out a long breath. "I won't be the last thug to come knocking after your guest, old man. But I promise I'll be the only polite one."

The innkeeper dabbed a towel across his forehead. "I suppose you've done away wit' my bouncers."

"They'll be fine," Shane said. "We're not throat cutters."

The women glanced at one another with wide eyes and pursed their lips at the open insult about Drawlen agents. They bent their heads and resumed chopping.

Pointing to a narrow servants' staircase, the innkeeper grumbled as he added the vegetables to his pot on the hearth.

Shane and Carris slipped through the kitchen and crept up the stairs to the second floor. The thrum of activity in the front room rattled the walls. Hopefully, this meant Kritcher hadn't heard the bell or the fight in the alley.

Approaching the door to the corner room, Shane slowed his breathing. He locked eyes with Carris and nodded. She returned the gesture and spun, kicking the door off its hinges before ducking out of the way.

A gun fired, the tang of red powder filling the air. The round shot breezed past Shane's shoulder. He ripped a sunrock lantern from the plastered wall, hurling it through the door. Another shot fired.

Carris launched herself over the threshold. A man screamed.

"Clear!" she called.

Shane sucked in a breath, glad this mad hunt could finally end. When he entered the room, he growled.

Carris knelt on the floor, clawed hand gripping the neck of a man pressed against the bed. In dress, build, and ethnicity, he matched their target. He'd even painted a mole on his right cheek to imitate Daeven Kritcher.

"Who the fires are you?" Shane demanded.

"A-an actor," the man sputtered. "Please, I had no idea"—he squeaked when Carris tightened her grip—"no idea Freelanders were after my client. The riots closed the theater. I'm just trying to pay my bills, you see."

Shane tugged his cloth cap tighter onto his head. He tucked in his loose silver braid, a feature clearly marking him a Zereen troll—not a welcome sight in the outlands. "Where's your client?"

"I don't know, truly. He paid me and left."

"With no security holding?" Shane raised a brow.

"I-I—" the man stammered.

Carris chuckled. "Thurse can smell lies, whelp. Best you tell this man the truth."

"He's—" The man groaned. "He's at the docks. He's getting on a ship."

"Atta boy," Carris said, choking him out with her sinewy arm. He slumped on the ground. The echo of activity downstairs shook the floor.

"Ha!" she barked, looking at the unconscious man. "Burning fool pissed himself."

"Let's go," Shane said. "Maybe Marcus will catch Kritcher at the docks."

She shrugged. "Or maybe that filth hired other *actors* and duped him, too."

"Sometimes I hate this job." Shane snarled.

2

EVASION

Corre, Agenom
April 14, 1190 PT

Shane

The city of Corre hugged a narrow bay leading west to the Cathyn Sea. Unlike the mountain-rimmed metropolis of Palim, where Shane spent most of his time, Corre lay on a flat expanse with rolling hills and vast fields falling away to the east. However, these two port cities shared one thing: the docks attracted the best and worst of characters.

Shane stepped onto the wharf when a girl brushed against him, reaching into his pocket. He caught her arm, growled with bared teeth, and sent her whimpering away, empty-handed. He stared after her. His chest twinged. He'd known too many like her.

A few yards down the boardwalk, a team of policemen on horseback escorted a gilded carriage that stopped at a luxury yacht called the *Fairy's Delight*. After the driver opened the door, an old woman in a red dress exited. When her dull-brown eyes, heavy with makeup, met Shane's, she blanched. She stuck up her nose and sauntered onto the boat, her bulky red skirts gathered in her hands.

A bell tolled throughout the district, marking the ninth hour. The last whisper of daylight sank over the watery horizon. Beyond the *Fairy's Delight*, Shane spotted Marcus Tolsum talking with a tawny dock worker. Having tucked his gold-weaved braids inside his cloth cap, Marcus blended with the Aginomians, only distinguishable by his long face and black eyes.

For this reason, Shane had assigned him to the docks. Aginomians were more likely to be helpful to someone they took as their own. The dock worker, stooping with a burlap sack slung across his shoulders, pointed toward the mouth of the harbor.

Marcus frowned, then nodded and marched toward Shane and Carris.

As he came closer, he spoke mentally through his mind craft. *'Kritcher is on a ship to Ostus. It left an hour ago.'*

Shane gnawed on his knuckles to stifle a string of curses. Carris shook her head.

Marcus reached them, brow furrowed while he glanced at the dock workers. Gray and black scruff covered his cheeks and jaw. Palish terrion typically stayed clean-shaven, but the last week of this manhunt had been relentless. "Three dock workers all told me they saw a fellow matching Kritcher's description boarding a cargo ship called the *Atlas*. The harbormaster says it usually runs between here and Hasava in Thura. It stops in Ostus to resupply."

Carris growled. "It's one thing to chase this fool across Palimar. Quite another to go to Thura."

"We might catch him in Ostus," Marcus offered, huffing.

"What if he gives us another slip?" Carris grumbled. "You gonna chase him to Thura, Tolsum? You'll get your wings clipped and your brain drilled into. At worst, they'll slice you up for dinner."

"Liiesh said . . ." Marcus began.

Shane put up a hand. "That burning spire lord can go there himself if he wants."

"I could overtake the ship," Marcus said. "On the open sea, I could claim a blood debt on Kritcher."

"You gonna fly that lump back here or something?" Carris asked with a laugh.

"I could wait on the ship and hire a return vessel in Ostus. The terrion there recognize Palish law." He tapped the breast pocket of his coat, where his coins clanged. "And money."

Shane scratched at the patchy silver stubble growing on his jaw. "It's not the worst plan. But you'll be too far to send word back if something goes wrong."

Marcus smirked. "I'll manage."

"And if he's not on that ship?" Carris asked.

"I'll fly back and meet you," Marcus said. "We'll have to put a foreign bounty on him. Even Thuran guns for hire don't balk at a Freelander payment. They know we're good for it."

Shane pursed his lips and gazed at the glassy, black water of the harbor. A natural breaker separated the port from the churning sea, a narrow mouth offering access to ships. "Fly. We'll wait at the inn . . . if it's still standing."

Marcus nodded. "I'll find you."

Up and down the wharf, dock workers continued their tasks under the blue light of tall sunrock lanterns placed along the water. They stuck to their work, paying no mind to Shane's crew.

"Try to lay low," Marcus said with a wink. In an instant, his great black wings materialized behind him, and he leapt into the sky. The rush of wind in his wake ruffled Shane's hat.

A few nearby workers gasped and pointed. Marcus glided above the water, the strong flap of his wings sending him steadily higher until he blended with the black sky, even to Shane's keen eyes.

Shane placed a hand on his goblin companion's shoulder. "Let's get some sleep."

With a shrug, Carris followed him along the slick, rotting planks of the boardwalk. When they passed the dock workers, one of them bent over and retched on the ground. A commotion of hollers halted their work.

Gripping his head, the sick man flopped at Shane's feet. When he turned his neck, his pupils dilated and retracted in quick succession.

Shane yanked Carris back as she stepped around the man with an annoyed grumble. "Hold up."

"You a doctor all the sudden?" Carris asked, her alto voice laced with sarcasm.

"He's having a seizure," Shane said. "From mind craft."

A teenage goblin boy wearing a gold indenture collar knelt next to the convulsing man. As the cloud cover rolled away, the two half-moons glowed, the red Mortemus twice the size of its silvery-blue neighbor, Vitaeus.

"Mateo," the boy said, shaking the convulsing man.

"He'll be fine in a minute," Shane said.

The boy leaned back, eyeing Shane with his mouth agape.

Sure enough, the man on the ground stilled and groaned. He mumbled in Aginomian.

"What's he saying?" Shane asked.

The boy met Shane's gaze with wide lavender eyes. "He's saying an old woman put magic on 'im."

"Old woman?" Shane asked.

Bending down, the boy spoke again with the man in his native tongue.

"An old woman in a red dress put pictures in his mind," he said to Shane. "Something about a man with a mole on his cheek getting on a ship." The boy rose and dragged the man to his feet. A few dock workers gathered around and carried him away.

"Fires in hell," Carris growled. "Someone used mind craft on this fellow. Deception. Kritcher does have an accomplice. Terrion, most likely."

"No," Shane said. "Kritcher apparently has his own mind craft. He disguised himself. Damn. I looked him right in his filthy eyes and didn't see him. Burning fires." He stared at the dock where the *Fairy's Delight* had been anchored moments ago. By now, it had cleared the harbor, its full sails catching the air stream, speeding it out to sea.

Marcus would be miles away by now, heading west while the ship Kritcher had actually boarded sailed north.

Carris pointed to a schooner docked halfway down the wharf. Worn silver letters reading *Sun Chaser* stood out against the peeling black tar paint on the stern. "That one looks fast. Maybe we can catch him."

Shane and Carris abandoned the crowd of murmuring dock men and ran to the *Sun Chaser*.

"Oi!" Carris called. "Anyone aboard?"

"You lookin' ta rob my ship, shorty?" said a gruff voice from the opposite side of the boardwalk.

A gangly human man with an ivory complexion leaned on the doorframe of a storage shed, one of many lining the dock.

"Lookin' for a ride," Carris said.

The man smiled, his thin lips lined with deep, red cracks as if he'd stayed too long in the sun. "I's the captain. And I's take yer money, or—" he looked Carris up and down.

Carris rolled her eyes. "I'm a biter," she said, clicking her pointed teeth.

The man grinned, revealing a missing front tooth. "Sounds fun."

"We pay well," Shane said, stepping forward. "Double if you'll leave now."

"Got no crew 'til morning," the man said. "I'll round 'em up nice 'n early fer four hundred."

"Tallies?" Carris barked.

"Each," the man replied.

Scoffing, Carris shook her head. "Sovereign's grace, that's a racket."

"Half now," Shane said. "Half at the destination."

"Which be?" the man asked.

"Wherever the *Fairy's Delight* is headed."

The captain pulled a pick from his pocket and stuck it between his teeth. "That be Estbye, way up north. That be double. I's headed to Port Selta otherwise."

Carris grumbled, but Shane interrupted. "First light, we're out of the harbor."

Shrugging, the man twirled the toothpick with his tongue. "Fine payday fer me. You two got a deal."

"Just one passenger," Shane said. "It's still plenty for you."

"Zem'Arta," Carris said in protest.

Shane turned to her. "Marcus will be back by morning. You stay here."

"Then what?" she asked.

"Then head to Setmal. Check in with Novelen. I'll meet you there."

Carris jeered. "With Daeven Kritcher in a sack?"

"Probably a box," Shane said.

"Or maybe an urn." She jabbed his shoulder with a finger. "You're no good solo, boy."

"Have a little faith in me, Mrs. Yan," he replied with a grin.

"Don't you dare call me. . ." She trailed off when Shane patted her shoulder. Jerking out of his reach, she brushed her sleeve and mumbled incoherently. Then she poked his lapel. "You be burning careful, boy."

"You too, elf."

"Why you flaming lunk—"

Shane's laughter drowned out her cursing. His amusement ended in a yawn.

"You should get some rest," Carris said. "And a map. Estbye is a tricky city."

"I know," he said, his mood darkening. He kept his face neutral though. He'd think on those sour memories later. "I've been there."

A knowing look darkened her sharp features. "With Henrick?"

"With Henrick," he said, the name bitter on his tongue.

⚬━┓

Morning came slowly, traces of pale light dancing on the eastern horizon. By the time threads of orange and purple wove into the sky, the *Sun Chaser* crossed the mouth of the harbor, turning north with a steady wind propelling her onward.

Shane leaned on the rail of the main deck. He dipped his hand into his shirt collar and pulled out the delicate wedding band that hung from a thin silver chain around his neck. Almost a year without her, and the pain from her loss still felt as fresh as that first day.

He stuffed the ring under his collar, forcing himself to think of better things. He slipped his hands into his pockets and spun around, putting his back to the railing and the rising sun. He flinched, his thumb brushing against soft parchment in his pocket. In the chase after Kritcher, he'd forgotten about the letter.

He pulled it out and unfolded the paper. Though stained and wrinkled, he could still read his friend's scrawl, could interpret her misspelling and her subtle code.

Dear Wolf,

We hope yer doing well. Thanks for yer last letter. Were happy yer taking good care of are brother. I'm shure it's a chor. We're doing well. Runs have been ful and buzy. I got to see some new citys. Some wer . . . better then others. Mom and dad say helo. We wish you could visit. We want to here yer stories in person. Espesialy sinse nothing intresting has hapened hear lately. You'll be happy to no that the most resent delivry of Sharling trade went horibly for them, thanks to the man in charg. That's it for now.

Al our best,

Mouse and Trickster

3

STAKEOUT

Estbye, Taria
April 24, 1190 PT

Ella

A bulky practice lock lay on the black table before Ella Therman, bump keys and spare picks scattered around it. As she twisted the lock picks a quarter turn, she bit her bottom lip. A familiar resistance arose within the contraption. Separating the two picks a fraction, she felt the release of the mechanism.

When a chill settled on her left shoulder, she hollered and jumped, the picks crunching into the lock as she jerked her hands away.

"Fires and—Illania!" she shouted upon seeing the pale, slender hand.

The young woman next to Ella giggled in her sultry way, twirling her long fingers with brightly painted nails. "This place could be on fire, and you wouldn't notice while you're working a lock," Illania said, a glint of amusement in her puffy eyes.

She pulled her other hand from her pocket, revealing a gilded switchblade. A handsome invention, it boasted gold filigree along a wooden handle.

"What's this?" Ella asked.

"An early birthday present." Illania cocked her head and tugged on the edges of Ella's ragged brown coat. "Truly, I'd like to give you a full makeover, but we'll start with accessories. Happy fifteen."

Ella chuffed and accepted the knife, stowing it in one of her many coat pockets. "Thanks. I'll let you know if I ever need fashion advice."

"The Devourer's Waste will grow roses before that happens." Illania sagged into the chair across from Ella and yawned, resting her elbows on the table and cradling her face in her hands. Curlers wound with shiny blonde hair framed her heart-shaped face. Ella rarely saw the young rogue without powdered cheeks and ruby-red lipstick. Illania favored theatrics and perfection, especially in her appearance.

"Late night?" Ella asked.

Illania yawned again and nodded. "Smuggling isn't really my game. And your old man is a touch pushy when it comes to his work. He expects me to watch the docks all night and get up with the sun to run his ridiculous errands."

"You volunteered for this, Miss Bradley," bellowed Jon's voice from the kitchen door. Ella's father leaned on the doorframe, gazing into the great room at the two girls. He lifted a steaming mug of coffee to his lips. Dark circles rimmed his brown eyes, and his beard stuck out at odd angles. They'd been shorthanded for this run, so he'd hired Illania to fill in.

The rogue leaned back and stretched her arms above her head. "Your terms were misleading, Therman."

Jon smirked, pulled out a chair, and leaned back. "No glamour or prestige. Hard work. Good pay. How is that misleading?"

"I'll remember that next time." Illania shrugged. "Still, it's nice to get out of Rotira now and then."

"Now and then?" Ella twirled the lock picks in her fingers. "One visit was enough for me. I'd prefer just about anywhere else."

"I thought you liked cities," Illania cooed while tightening a curler in her hair.

Ella scoffed and pushed the practice lock aside. "I like cities that aren't ruled by drug runners."

With a hum, Illania replied, "You prefer cities run by tyrannical immortals?"

Wrinkling her brow, Ella shook her head. "You may have a point. At least the immortals keep their streets clean."

Jon scratched his beard. "The tax man in Estbye is easier to evade than Rotiran thugs running a protection racket."

"Aren't you related to those Rotiran thugs?" Illania asked.

Jon opened his mouth to answer when Cameron entered the room from the front hall door. The den, as Ella and her fellow smugglers called it, appeared as an unassuming storefront near the lower docks. A shop room stocked with dry goods occupied the front of the building. A hallway led into the great room that served as the Estbye headquarters for their smuggling network.

Cameron, a stout woman with a weathered face, twitched her hand closer to her belt where a bulky purse hid her miniature pistol. A loaded gun within arm's reach was her constant companion.

"What is it?" Jon asked, staring intently at the guarded look on the older woman's face.

"There's a man asking for"—she paused, clearing her throat—"transportation."

Jon narrowed his eyes. "He knows what he's asking for?"

"Seems so," Cameron said. "He's alone. Don't know 'im. Came by ship."

Jon rose from his seat, leaving his coffee untouched. "I'll bring him to the office."

"Need backup?" Illania asked.

"Yes," Jon said, "but he'll speak more freely if he doesn't know he's outnumbered."

Illania bounced from her seat with newfound energy and skipped to Ella's side. "I love eavesdropping. Come on."

Swept up in her friend's high spirits, Ella bounded toward the office door adjacent to the hallway. The office, a windowless space, sat nestled between the storefront and the great room with a door to each. The girls hid in the corner.

The air chilled as Illania summoned a shade. It appeared as a black, formless mass roughly the size of a man. Most people, other than ralenta like Illania, couldn't see these specters without significant practice. Perhaps because of Ella's parentage, she had always been able to see shades, though she possessed no shade craft.

The apparition stretched from wall to wall, becoming transparent. The room, formerly bright and warm, became darker and colder as the shade wrapped Illania and Ella in a cocoon of invisibility.

Illania clicked her tongue and patted her hair curlers. "I wish I'd taken the time to get ready."

Ella squeaked in laughter. "No one can see you right now. What does it matter?"

Illania pursed her lips disapprovingly. "What if he causes trouble and I have to intervene?" She gestured to her pale bedclothes. "Do you think he'll take a fright to an unkempt woman in this sack?"

"I think he'll take a fright to the shades strangling him, no matter what you're wearing."

Illania sucked in a breath but shut her mouth as the storefront door opened. Jon entered first, glancing toward the corner where the girls hid. Knowing he could only see a deep shadow, a thrill buzzed through Ella, the anticipation of intrigue. Her imagination strayed when a stranger entered the room. Who could he be? How could he have known to come here and use their code?

Jon stepped behind the desk and sat in the tall-backed leather chair. He leaned to one side, placing his hand—covered in a fingerless glove— under his chin. Again he swept his brown eyes to where Ella and Illania hid, then back at the older man taking a seat before the desk.

"Well, Mr. Herold," Jon said.

The pale man scratched at his graying temples. He may have been a handsome man in his youth, minus the ugly mole dominating his right cheek. His nose, beet red and infested with spider veins, told of a life of heavy drinking.

The man's words cut through Ella's musing. "Just Herold, Master Taff," he said, using Jon's alias. Dressed in the frills and accessories of high fashion, Herold may have passed for an aristocrat to the untrained observer.

But the fraying lace of his cuff and collar and the fabric's cheap texture betrayed him. He did have the straight-backed posture for a highborn man, however. Perhaps he'd been one once and had fallen on hard times. Or perhaps he'd indebted himself to the wrong people. This wouldn't be the first desperate noble Jon Therman spirited away.

Jon grunted and leaned forward. "All right, Herold. Most folk come here looking for bulk goods."

Herold arched a fine gray brow. "Most people, I'm sure, don't come here at all."

"We do most of our business at the docks," Jon replied in a deadpan tone.

"You're smugglers," Herold said plainly. "And I need something smuggled. Must we keep on with the innuendo?"

"What led you to that conclusion?" Jon asked, a smirk tugging at his thin lips.

"I arrived in Estbye on the *Fairy's Delight*. Captain Bellamy said—"

Jon cut him off with a chuckle. "You don't need something smuggled. You need yourself smuggled."

The man blinked a few times, his mud-brown eyes widening. "Well . . . yes. I seem to be in an unfortunate situation. You see, I've had a falling out with a business partner. He was not content with the half profits of our latest venture. I have a small fortune, but he'd see to it that I have nothing left but the clothes on my back. You really must believe me."

Jon put up his hands. "I don't give a damn about your situation, Herold. Can you pay?"

"What's your price?"

"Depends where I'm taking you," Jon said.

"Pelton," Herold said. "I have friends there."

The hairs on Ella's neck prickled, a chill weaving down her spine. She doubted Herold had anything close to friends in the Corigish capital. She doubted everything about the man, especially his name.

"The *Fairy's Delight* came from Corre," Jon said. "And you want to go halfway back?"

Herold plucked his wide brimmed hat from his head and fidgeted with it. Rather than twitching and shaking, as a truly nervous man might, Herold's action seemed more forced, mechanical.

He's acting, Ella thought.

"As I said," Herold began. "I have friends in Pelton. I couldn't go by land from Corre for . . . reasons."

"Reasons," Jon repeated, pursing his lips. "Well, if you need to get to Pelton discreetly, Captain Bellamy sent you to the right people."

"We can leave now?" Herold said, sitting up taller. Ella perceived his statement and eagerness as genuine. He may have been lying about his circumstances, but he definitely wanted out of Estbye.

"Not in such short order," Jon said. "And we haven't discussed your payment schedule yet."

"I really am in a hurry," Herold said.

"We leave in two days," Jon said. "No sooner."

"Two—two days?" Herold stammered.

Fear. A frightened liar. Jon's favorite type of client. They made for the biggest challenge. And the greatest risk.

"A hundred tallies now," Jon said. "A hundred when we get you to the capital."

Herold balked, then cleared his throat. "Seventy-five for the delay."

Ella pursed her lips to keep from laughing. No one bested Jon Therman at negotiation. No one.

He gazed at Herold in silence for a drawn-out moment. "Mr. Herold, do you want to get to Pelton in one piece, or would you rather go back to the Freelands in an urn?"

"The Freelands?" Herold said with a fake guffaw. "I've never been—"

Jon's chair groaned as he leaned to the side. "Native, I'd say, by your accent. Though you've done an admirable job hiding it. Your taste in purple embroidery is another tell. Only clerics wear that color around here."

Herold's face flushed and he gulped.

"You've nothing to fear from me, whoever you are," Jon said. "I have no love for any creed or country, only a paying customer. One hundred now, or I may raise my price."

Illania's shoulders shook with silent laughter. Ella chewed her bottom lip and smiled at her friend.

Herold sighed and dug into the purse at his belt. He placed ten tallies on the worn gray desk. "I'll have to make an exchange for the rest."

"You do that," Jon said. "I only take Drawlen currency."

Herold patted the pile of square coins, then rose and scrambled from the room. Jon waited silently, breathing slowly before glancing sidelong toward the corner.

As Illania withdrew her shade, the room brightened. "That was . . . not as fun as I was hoping," she said with a pout. "Good catch on the accent. I didn't pick up on that."

"Bellamy warned me last night," Jon said. "Also mentioned the man may have followers."

"The unfriendly type?" Illania asked.

"Yes," Jon said.

"And you took his money?"

"Yes."

Illania burst into laughter, folding in on herself. "Mother of dryads, Therman. You must be desperately bored to tempt fate with Freelanders."

"We'll leave tomorrow," Jon said. "If someone's after our new friend, we'll be well on the road before they give chase."

Ella licked her lips. "You said two days."

"I know what I said," Jon replied. "Mr. Herold will tell the innkeeper at the Knight's Rest, which will give whoever's trailing him the illusion of time, if that phantom pursuer even comes at all. The point being, Herold is too skittish to do this right. So we must do it for him."

Illania brushed her arm across her forehead in a mock swoon. "Brilliance! How did the Corigish underworld survive without you for four whole years?"

Ella's breath caught. Illania spoke casually about many serious topics. Jon's time in Langry prison had just become one of them.

"It's called networking. Ladies, we have work to do." Jon stuffed the ten tallies into a pouch and pointed at Illania. "Get dressed, quickly. You're going to make sure our new package doesn't get snatched." He stood and turned to Ella. "El, watch the docks. If another ship arrives from Corre, we can expect unfriendlies."

"And if I find any?" Ella asked.

Jon's gaze darkened. "Find out where they're staying and keep yourself out of trouble. Do *not* engage them, no matter what."

"Yes, Papa," Ella said.

Illania giggled and grabbed her hand, pulling her into a trace. The world turned black and frigid before a rush of freezing wind formed around her. Her lungs burned, and she braced herself on the dressing table in the room she shared with Illania.

Gripping her chest, Ella huffed in annoyance. "I burning hate when you do that!"

Illania chuckled and flung herself onto her unkempt bed. "Lighten up, Little Mouse."

Ella rolled her eyes. "I also hate that nickname." Tugging her ragged coat tightly around her, she strode to the door.

"Be careful," Illiana said in a serious tone. "A Freeland thug is as bad as a purifier, maybe worse."

Ella turned the doorknob. "Danger's never bothered me."

A pillow sailed toward her, shade smoke entangling it. Ella dodged with a laugh.

"I know," Illania said. "That's the trouble."

By early evening, Ella yearned for something interesting to happen. She hated stakeouts. Most often, they amounted to uneventful hours on cold nights. This one at least had taken place primarily under the sun, though the sea breeze still held a chill.

Ships came and went from the harbor, mostly from Port Selta and Ostus. The last ship, a transport galleon from the Crescent Isles, inched into the harbor with the setting sun casting its billowed sails in golden light. As she crossed the threshold of the harbor, the harbormaster blew his horn, signaling the final port call.

Ella rose from the bench she'd claimed earlier that day and headed toward the city. Estbye certainly was the most beautiful place in the world. Stacked tenements of ivory plaster crowned the hills and cliffs surrounding the harbor. Stout, round towers dominated the wealthy district overlooking the city, and seas of colorful tents populated the sprawling market squares.

The Drawlen temple, a cascading stack of bronze-gilded squares, clashed with its surroundings. Though the temple dwarfed most other buildings in the city, it appeared comically insignificant next to the Creedan cathedral across the neighborhood. Even from the docks, the Palim-influenced spires rose above the cathedral's domed roofline.

Of course, the building no longer served as a place of worship. Being over five hundred years old, it had been spared destruction by the conquering Drawls on a strange technicality. The Drawlen clerics had come with their hoards two centuries ago and had claimed Taria in the name of the Corigish crown without so much as a single battle.

The Drawlen-appointed lord of Estbye had been a descendant of the cathedral's architect and chose to keep it as his family's estate. That estate had floundered, and the cathedral had changed hands among the city's elite in the past few decades.

Adjusting her lapel, Ella marched toward the square. Another horn call halted her. She turned back. As the transport galleon floated toward her dockings, a black speck on the horizon emerged. Another ship. A small ship.

Ella hustled to reach the harbormaster. A gangly man in his thirties, his dark skin and tightly curled hair put him out of place among the pale Tarish natives.

"Is that the ship you seek, young lady?" he asked in a light tSolani accent.

"No," Ella said with confidence, masking her lie with a smile. She tucked a brown curl behind her ear. "My friend was coming on a bigger ship, I'm sure. I'll come back tomorrow."

She walked off at an even pace. Her whole body buzzing with energy, she knew this ship meant something to her mission. She had told the harbormaster that she expected a friend from Corre. She'd given him no more details, not wanting to tip off Herold's hunter more than necessary.

She feigned heading toward the square. When she rounded the corner, she slipped into an alley and found a secluded spot with a view of the schooner now entering the harbor. The boat glided along the dock before the harbormaster.

"Where you hail from?" he called.

Two men leaned on the deck rail, one a short, skinny fellow, the other tall and stocky.

"Corre, Aginom, good sir," the short man answered.

"Stock to report?" the harbormaster asked.

"Silk and cotton, sir, and one passenger." The captain pointed to the tall man next to him.

The passenger flashed a small object toward the harbormaster and spoke in tSoli. His accent sounded wrong, but the harbormaster chuckled and replied in his native tongue.

Immediately, the tall man leapt from the ship onto the wharf and patted the harbormaster's shoulder, placing something in his hand.

Ella tensed. Had the harbormaster given her up? She glanced around, figuring her best route if the man gave chase.

She relaxed when he stalked off in the opposite direction. Her relief quickly gave way to a buzz of anticipation. Slinking from her hiding place, she followed him. As she passed a vendor stall, she purchased a sack of mealy apples. Swinging the sack onto her back, she pulled a flat cap from an inner coat pocket.

The man she trailed twitched his head to the side, glancing behind him. Shoving the cap on her head, she ducked into an alcove. She peered around the wall, only to find him gone.

"Fires," she muttered. She strode casually along the boardwalk, hoping to glimpse him without garnering suspicion. At the junction of a side street crowded with crates and barrels, she spied his profile.

Before he turned another corner, she spotted his olive face and silver hair poking out under his flat cap. A Freelander for certain, and possibly a troll, given his skin tone. Dangerous, indeed.

Something about the man gave her pause. Sucking in a breath, she trailed him. Again, she lost sight of her quarry. A quiver ran up her back. She dropped the apple sack. She, the hunter, had become the hunted. Somewhere he watched her, hidden, sinister, knowing. She bolted.

— 4 —

REUNION

Estbye, Taria
April 24, 1190 PT

Ella

As Ella veered onto the wharf, she toppled a stack of crates to cover her escape. A string of curses in a low, gravelly voice sounded behind her. She sprinted, weaving through the few dozen bystanders and dock workers. Shouts from onlookers, along with her pursuer's growling voice, told her the man remained close on her heels.

Slipping a hand into her pocket, she gripped her gifted switchblade and stole a glimpse at the man. He inched close enough for her to see the vertical shape of his pupils, to confirm her fear: a Zereen troll, a member of the infamous Freelander warrior clan.

She sputtered a curse as he extended a clawed hand. Throwing her weight to the side, she twirled out of his reach and opened the knife. In one fluid motion, she slashed the blade across his forearm, cutting his coat sleeve and slicing flesh. She landed as he flinched and tumbled in the opposite direction, regaining himself on the edge of the dock.

Ella hurtled forward with her leg outstretched, her boot striking the man in the chest. He grunted, opening his mouth wide to reveal his sharp teeth. Three faint scars marred his cheeks—two on the left, one on the right.

A familiar face flashed in her memory—one with only two scars.

"Shane?" she blurted while balancing on the edge of the planks.

He hit the water with an oily splash.

"Oh fires," Ella said. "Oh—" A commotion distracted her. Two policemen, distinguishable by their brown uniforms and red belts, rounded the bend and pointed their batons at Ella.

"Oh fires, oh fires!" She bolted in the opposite direction. What choice did she have?

The officers proved far easier to evade than, well, *him*. Had it truly been him? Around a corner, down an alley, up a wall, over a low roof, and she'd shaken the officers. She slipped gracefully from the roof and turned back toward the docks, only to slam into a hard, wet, leather-clad chest.

She jumped back with a shout. Eyes like a clear sky bore into hers. She no longer doubted. Shane stood before her, bent forward with his mouth curled into a sinister smirk. But his gaze held no recognition, only malice and triumph.

"Caught you," he snarled.

A whistle shrilled overhead. One of the policemen stood on a nearby roof, pointing at them with his baton.

"I see them!" he called. "The girl and the ogre."

Shane growled at the slur.

The man on the roof pulled a pistol from his belt.

Ella yanked Shane's wrist, slick with seawater and blood. "Quick! Follow me," she said as she ran.

"What the hell?" he called out.

"They'll introduce you to Drawlen collectors if they catch you," Ella said.

Shane ran after her. She ducked around vendor stalls and along covered alcoves, hoping her unexpected companion could keep up. He moved with the grace and speed of a much smaller man. He'd always been agile, as she recalled, and menacing.

Four more officers appeared at the other end of the crowded street, hollering at them. Ella backstepped, recalculating her route. She squealed when Shane seized her arm and yanked her back the way they'd come.

"Not that way!" Ella yelled and wriggled free of his grasp.

Sure enough, the first two officers cut them off at the junction. Without hesitation, Shane slammed an elbow into the shorter man's face, knocking him down. The other man thrust his baton, which Shane dodged and snatched away. After Shane pummeled him with four hard blows from his own weapon, the officer sank to his knees and keeled over.

Shane leapt past him. Ella followed, struggling to keep up.

"Wait," she pleaded.

He led her onto a wide street alongside a canal, right in front of a police station teaming with officers changing shifts for the night.

"Damn," Shane muttered as a whistle sounded behind him.

Ella threw up her hands. "See what I mean?" She pulled him by his sleeve just as the other pursuing officers arrived. Weaving corner after corner, Ella sprinted with Shane at her heels through a wealthy neighborhood woven with canals. The officers fell behind but remained in pursuit.

Seeing a passing boat occupied only by a helmsman, Ella shoved Shane forward. "Jump!"

With bulging eyes, he hesitated before leaping onto the boat. As Ella sprang toward the vessel, she flung a handful of silver marks at the nearby crowd. They groped for the falling coins and smiled when she put a finger to her lips. After landing on the boat, she handed a few marks to the helmsman. He pocketed them and winked at her. Just as the officers arrived on the street along the waterway, the boat passed under a high, arching bridge.

Ella hopped onto a ledge under the bridge, motioning for Shane to follow. They pressed themselves against the arching underside as a policeman yelled to the crowd, "Have you seen a girl in a brown coat? And a troll?"

"Not around here," someone answered.

"Who the fires are you?" Shane whispered to Ella, his eyes narrowing.

"Just a little mouse out for a stroll," Ella said as she pulled off her cap.

His face contorted. His azure eyes widened, his mouth going slack before turning up in a smile.

He resumed his grim expression when one of the policemen yelled, "Where the bloody burning fires did those whelps go?"

The other officer mumbled an inaudible reply, and the *tap, tap, tap* of their footfalls on the stone faded.

After a moment, a child poked his head through the rungs on the bridge railing and whispered, "They're gone."

Ella waved at the boy. He giggled. Another canal boat glided under the bridge with a helmsman escorting a young couple.

As Ella hopped onto their narrowboat, the startled pair sprang apart. The woman, her head piled with decadent brown curls, squeaked when Shane followed.

Squatting onto the bench, Ella handed the helmsman a gold tally coin, a handsome price for stowing them away. With a bow, he accepted the payment and went back to steering the vessel. Ella smiled at the couple.

"Fine evening," she said.

"L-lovely," the man stuttered. He gawked at Shane, sucking in a breath.

Shane glowered back. His silver braid dangled from his flat cap, draping down his arm. Seawater dripped from the two gray drake teeth strung at the end of his braid. Tarish folk knew little of the world beyond their borders. But silver-haired trolls with drake tooth trophies had become household legends—and horror stories.

The woman opened her mouth as if to speak, letting it hang as she stared past Ella. In the fleeting light of evening, the Creedan cathedral came into view. Purple light kissed the edges of its black spires and sweeping domes. The stained glass windows, depicting scenes from the Psalm of the Serenity Creed, shone unusually bright.

The tall double doors stood open, a procession of finely dressed men and women filing in. On the street, a crowd lingered before the front steps under crisscrossing strings of sun crystals. Ella would have to come back later to see about filching some of them.

As the boat scraped along the bricks bordering the canal, the couple disembarked hastily, then scurried into the throng.

"Where to, miss?" the helmsman asked.

"South market," Ella said.

Shane stared into the crowd, a dark gleam in his eyes. Ella followed the Zereen's gaze. The swarm of wealthy couples parted for a gilded carriage drawn by four sleek gray horses. On the door, an octagon formed the window with a cutout of the eight-sided Star of Sovereign—the symbol of Drawlen.

Two graycoats, members of the Drawlen military, occupied the driver's bench. A green-clad footman leapt from the back of the carriage and swung open the door. Applause from the throng accompanied the woman exiting the coach.

Her black locks, piled high, accentuated her pale, pointed ears. Fae. A fae without an indenture collar and riding in a Drawlen carriage only meant one thing.

"Immortal," Shane muttered, lips twitching into a snarl.

"South market," Ella repeated to the helmsman, whose eyes lingered on the beautiful woman.

Now he blanched and pushed the boat away from the cathedral.

After the immortal bowed to her audience, she shifted her attention toward the boat. Her eyes narrowed. Ella stood and pointed ahead, hoping to Sovereign her position blocked Shane from the woman's view. The fae turned back to the crowd and glided toward the cathedral steps, the surrounding gentry falling in behind her.

Ella let out a long breath as she sank onto the bench. "Your braid," she whispered to Shane.

His brows creased for a second before his hand snapped to his shoulder. He stuffed his hair back into his soaked hat. Blood dripped from the stain on his sleeve down his wrist.

"Sorry about the cut," Ella said.

Shane examined his arm and shrugged. "Barely a scratch."

"A scratch that might need stitches."

"You offering?"

Ella bumped her shoulder into his. "If you're polite."

"Never mind, then," Shane said. He smiled, his eyes glinting along with his sharp teeth.

The boat glided around a wide point, coming into view of the Drawlen temple. Whereas the native architecture of Estbye consisted of sweeping rooflines, stucco, and squat towers, the Drawls favored marble walls and hard lines.

The building clashed so much that its potential beauty suffered. Ella's disdain for the Drawlen regime also took away from the building's appeal. A group of priestesses in green robes, women of the Order of Eruna, sprinkled oil on the heads of kneeling worshippers.

Not just any worshippers. Every face in the crowd bore deep wrinkles and sunken eyes—elderly citizens destined for the urn, or . . .

She grimaced and turned her head as the boat glided by.

"What are they doing?" Shane asked in a somber tone.

"Preparing for the Life Harvest," Ella said in a low voice. "If they die in the next few weeks, they'll be burned. If not, they'll be taken to Drawl for, well, you know."

Shane scoffed and spit into the water. "That's messed up."

The helmsman hummed in agreement.

Silence blanketed the boat, other than the gentle splash of the wake. When the boat rounded a bend, Shane leaned forward, meeting Ella's gaze.

"I thought you ditched this town."

"I'm working," Ella said. "I thought you hated the outlands."

Shane smirked. "I'm working."

"Does your work involve chasing a man from Corre?"

Shane's shoulders sagged. "How—how do you know that?"

"A man calling himself Herold asked for our help in . . . transportation to Pelton. He came from Corre."

"Mole on his right cheek?" Shane asked.

"That's the one."

Shane shook his head. "Burning fires."

Ella dipped her hand in the water. "Why are you after him?"

"Let's say he's wanted by some important people in the Freelands."

"Wanted enough to send you all the way out here?"

Shane propped his elbows on his knees. "I can't fail on this one, El, even if it means robbing you of a job."

Ella flicked water at him, causing him to flinch. "We'll work something out. In the meantime, let's get you dried off."

Shane growled, scooping a handful of water and splashing her.

She laughed, scrubbing her face with her sleeve.

After a few minutes, the helmsman steered the boat along the edge of the canal and tipped his hat. "Here you are, lady."

Ella stood and slipped him another tally coin. "We weren't here."

"No, ma'am. Not a sight of ya."

Replacing her cap, Ella stepped onto the street. Shane followed. Under the blue glow of the sunrock streetlamps, they skittered from the canal. A green-robed priest brushed past them, scurrying in the direction of the temple.

Shane watched him disappear around a building. "How can you stand it, living under the thumb of deranged immortals?"

Ella shrugged, her gaze locking on the two criminal marks marring his left cheek. "I imagine it's not much different than how you tolerate working for the man who marked you."

Shane froze mid-stride and stared at her. "I see your point. So, you hate every minute of it."

"In their presence," Ella admitted, pausing beside him. "That's why I live in the middle of nowhere. No immortal has ever been to Lorinth, and no immortal ever will."

Shane snorted. "So, I should live in a hole in the ground far from any city. Is that it?"

Ella shoved him. Or tried to. He stood, unmoved by her half-hearted assault. "I don't live in a hole," Ella said.

"It's in the ground," Shane said. "It counts."

"Jerk," Ella muttered, swatting his arm.

They continued through the market in silence. Most of the vendors had cleared their stalls. A rat scampered across the street in front of Ella, causing an old woman nearby to screech.

Ella glanced at Shane, working up the courage to ask her nagging question. Before she opened her mouth, he spoke.

"Your brother's fine," he said. "And annoying."

Ella laughed. "Not annoying enough for you to boot him from your crew."

Shane muffed her hair. "He's useful."

"That's a high compliment, coming from you."

Huffing, Shane fell into silence once more. They left the market, heading south.

"How are your parents?" he asked after a few minutes. "And the boys?"

"Papa's here," Ella said.

"Sounds rosy."

Ella drew in a breath. "Some days are better than others. It's a big adjustment, being out in the world after, well, after Langry prison."

"He's lucky to be alive," Shane said.

"Yeah," she agreed. "Krishena put a five-thousand-tally bounty on anyone who might hurt him. That pretty much put everyone in there on his side."

Passing a beggar rattling a tin cup, Shane slipped him a silver mark. "Clever. How about Ruth?"

"Mom's okay. She gets stir-crazy sometimes, not being able to leave town. They don't make her wear an indenture collar in Lorinth though, so that's nice. We got a new priest, Emerel Ferren. Way better than the old one. He treats mom like a proper physician."

"Still a slave though," Shane said in a bitter tone.

Ella pursed her lips. "Yeah." After an awkward silence, she added, "The boys are good. Nate started apprenticing with the town blacksmith."

"Waste of his talent," Shane said. "He was born for espionage."

"Please." Ella groaned. "Mom would cry."

"I'm just saying . . ." Shane trailed off with a snicker. "Jeb's okay too? Kid would hardly come out of his room when I visited."

"You scared the poor boy!" Ella scolded. "You and that bodyguard, so broody and serious."

"They're all like that, with a few exceptions."

"Well, one was enough for Jeb."

They headed down a main street. A wall of posters greeted them, some advertising theater productions or street performances, others depicting fugitives. A wanted poster caught Ella's eye. She lifted the puppet show advertisement that obscured it.

"Fires," Shane said. "They still post those?"

Ella brushed her hand across her half-brother's face, or what the collectors meant to be his likeness. The features didn't quite match, though it still depicted Remm's dark skin and close-cropped hair—the face of a fourteen-year-old boy, eyes narrowed in the poor impression of evil.

"The nose is wrong," Shane said.

"Papa had his people switch the printing plates."

"From prison?"

Ella ripped the poster from the wall, folded it, and stuffed it into an inner pocket of her sagging coat. "He only stayed in that place so that we didn't have to live as fugitives. It almost broke him to send Remm away."

Shane's brow crinkled as he pushed his hands in his pockets. "I know it's not the same as having him home, but the kid landed on his feet."

Ella chuckled. "Kid? Aren't you the same age?"

Resting a hand on his chest, Shane said, "I'm a few years older and way more mature."

"Mature enough to gain another mark?"

Shane stroked his right cheek. For a second, his eyes darkened.

"Did the First Lord give you that one too?" Ella asked.

"No," Shane said. "I got this one . . . I'll tell you about it some other time."

"Sorry," Ella said, looking away. "I didn't mean to pry."

"It's fine. I had to choose between helping my brother or standing by while a scoundrel got away."

Ella snapped her head toward him. "You have a brother?"

"Two," Shane said. He hunched, his gaze straying to the ground.

"Oh." Ella didn't press further. Clearly a painful topic. She approached the storefront that hid the smuggler's den. A chipped and faded sign, its letters no longer legible, hung above the shabby door. "Here we are."

With a key from her pocket, she opened the door a fraction. Adjacent to the shop's entrance, the inside office door stood open. A gangly man lingered at the threshold, his profile partially obscured by his signature hat with a single feather propped on the side.

Raised voices wafted from the office, mostly Cameron's.

"Who's that?" Shane whispered.

"Mars Quinley," Ella said. "Our supplier."

"Fifty percent," Mars said in a shaking voice. "Or there's . . . there's no deal."

Ella opened the door fully. The tinkling of the bell above the door drowned out the creaking hinges.

"Who's there?" Cameron barked.

"It's El," she replied.

Jon appeared in the office doorway. "Any news?"

Ella glanced at Mars, who stood beside Jon, fiddling with his pocket watch.

"Herold has a visitor." She moved aside, and Shane stepped through the door.

As Shane entered the smuggler's den, Jon's hand twitched toward the pistol at his belt. He stilled, eyes widening. His mask of shock cracked into a shallow smile, his hands relaxing at his side. He nodded to Ella, a grin on his face. "Taking in strays again?"

○— 5 —○

OLD FRIENDS

Estbye, Taria
April 24, 1190 PT

Shane

Shane's chest contracted. Sorrow and tenacity mingled in Jon's brown eyes. When Shane had last seen him three years ago, Jon was still an inmate in Langry, a notorious prison north of Depbas. He'd insisted on seeing Jon after visiting Ruth and the children at the Therman farmstead.

"It's too dangerous," Varus, his gray-haired terrion escort, had said.

Shane, a crass, stubborn teenager at the time, had spat at Varus's feet. "You can help me see my friend, or you can fly home to the First Lord without me."

Varus acquiesced, pulling strings with the right people to get Shane into an interrogation room in Langry. The guards, gray-clad Drawlen rangers, shoved Jon onto the floor of the room and snatched the cowl off his head before slamming the door.

Jon had knelt with his eyes on the ground, fists clenched, shoulders tucked. "I'll say this once," he bit out. "The Rogue Master's bounty does not expire. You can have your fun, but the price is an eye and a hand. She always takes her due."

Shane leaned against the rough wall. "Sounds like my kinda woman."

Jon lifted his chin, his glare boring into Shane for a moment before his face contorted. His eyes narrowed at the two convict marks on Shane's face. "Who are you?"

"Just a stray," Shane said, harkening back to words Jon had once spoken to him.

Eyes widening, Jon leapt to his feet. "Boy?" He wiped his mouth, shaking his head. "Shane?"

Shane's lips cracked into a grin. "Hey, old man."

"What—how are you here?"

"You told me to find better friends. I sort of did."

Patting his own left cheek, Jon eyed Shane. "And a few enemies, it seems."

"You said I'd have to pay a pirate's bounty eventually," Shane said. "You were right."

"You ditched Henrick?" Jon asked, his tone low and guttural.

"Even burned his ship," Shane said. "He got away."

Jon rubbed his wrists. "Always does."

To still his shaking hands, Shane scratched the back of his neck. "You can get away, too, Jon. I saw Ruth and the kids. I could get you out. You could—"

Jon spread his arms. "I know it looks like they've beat me. This is just a setback."

"A six-year sentence?" Shane said. "That's one big setback."

"I don't plan to be here longer than four," Jon said. "Put a few tallies in the right hands, and I'll be out soon enough."

"Soon enough to what?" Shane scoffed. "To hang out in that shanty town while your wife wears an indenture collar for the next fourteen years? While your kids wait to be conscripted? Jon, the Drawlen territories will eat your family alive eventually! Come to the Freelands."

Jon shook his head. "So they can be subject to spire lords instead? How's that going for you?"

Shane flinched. "Think about it."

"How did you get in here?" Jon asked. "How did you get away from Henrick?"

In that moment, Shane could only gaze at the floor.

"You don't have the posture of a free man, zem'Arta," Jon said.

Shane clenched his fists, his body trembling. He had felt vulnerable and powerless, just like the very first time he'd met Jon. Slowly, he lifted his head. "If I'm not one man's pawn, I'm another's. I tried, Jon. I really did."

He had expected a retort, a sharp word. He shuddered when Jon strode forward and pulled him into a gentle embrace. Years had passed since a man had touched Shane without the threat of violence. He shook, his arms stiffening at his sides. He had forgone the opportunity to see his own father in favor of this man and his family. Even though Shane longed to see his father, Jon had made him believe that freedom was possible, had given him the courage to reach for it.

Now, standing in the cramped storefront of the smuggler's den in Estbye, Shane felt like that same angry, conflicted teenager. A lifetime of misfortune and regret threaded the three intervening years. He'd reunited with his own father since, but Jon remained among the few men Shane truly trusted.

Jon smiled warmly and extended his hand to Shane. When they clasped forearms, Shane patted him on the back.

"Good to see you, young man," Jon said.

Ella grasped her hands behind her back and rocked on her heels. Her eyes crinkled, giving away the smile she attempted to hide. Though she'd matured greatly in the past three years—now a young woman rather than a child—her gaze still held that innocent wonder. None of her life's tragedies, which numbered many, had robbed her of that welcoming, hopeful demeanor.

Mars Quinley, standing behind Jon, cleared his throat. "Perhaps I'll return in the morning." His voice held a nervous air, though his tone sounded forceful. "I trust you'll be more agreeable by then, Jon."

Stepping away from Shane, Jon addressed Mars. "Doubling your cut in the eleventh hour is no way to win friends."

"Circumstances have—" Mars hesitated a moment, rolling his pocket watch between his fingers. "They have changed. It's out of my control."

"You mean someone got yer ass over a fire?" barked the old woman standing next to Jon.

As she opened her mouth to speak further, Jon raised a hand. "It's all right, Cameron. Mr. Quinley has said his piece. We'll talk further in the morning, if his financial backers don't come to collect in the meantime."

Mars and Cameron sputtered in surprise. Ella's lips turned up in a smirk.

"What could you possibly mean?" Mars demanded. "You know I'm independent. It's just the economy, and the risks have—"

Jon clicked his tongue. "I'm not interested in your cover story. Who have you fallen in with?"

Mars's wide-eyed gaze settled on Shane, who raised a brow.

"A name," Jon said.

"H-Hellen," Mars muttered. "She's a . . . broker of sorts."

"Where can I find her?" Jon asked in an even tone.

"Tonight, I'd imagine she's at the cathedral gala."

Shane and Ella glanced at one another.

Cameron grumbled. "A highborn?"

"Pretends to be," Mars said. "Listen, Jon. We've been in business together a long time. This is not a woman you want to tangle with. She has her hand in many operations, both above board and below, and plenty of friends on both sides, if you catch me."

"And she's calling in debts?" Jon mused.

Mars nodded, the feather in his cap brushing the doorframe. "It seems so. I'm not the only one of her unfortunate retainers being squeezed right now."

Jon patted Mars's back. "We'll get this figured out. Go with Cameron to the back room. Tell her everything. Then get yourself tucked away somewhere this woman can't find you. I'll let you know when it's safe."

"Are you sure?" Mars asked. "This whole business may be beyond both of us."

"We'll find out. If it's too risky, we'll up the cut and pivot our business some other way in the future. Go. And send Bradley in here." Jon pointed to the back door of the office.

Cameron ushered Mars through and shut the door, leaving Jon, Shane, and Ella in the secluded office. Jon fixed on the mark marring Shane's right cheek. "Did Liiesh Romanus give you that one too?"

"No," Shane said. "Let's just say I'm not welcome at any more family reunions."

Jon sniffed, slouching into his office chair. "And what brings you back to Estbye?"

Shane pulled out a wobbly chair and straddled it. He ignored the sharp creak it made under his weight. "I'm here for your man, Herold."

Ella shrugged when Jon shifted his gaze to her. Then, his eyes fell on the bloody gash in Shane's forearm, visible through his torn sleeve. "You look like you swam here," Jon said.

Shane fiddled with the frayed fabric on his arm. "I took a dip."

Ella snickered behind her hand.

"Herold made a deposit," Jon said.

Shane draped his arms over the chairback. "You can keep it, but that slimy wretch comes with me."

"That may not suit my reputation if I just let you walk off with a man I've agreed to smuggle."

"You'll still be smuggling him," Shane said. "The only difference is who pays the bill."

"You'll have to do better than just pay his tab," Jon said.

Shaking his head with a smile, Shane asked, "What's your price?"

Jon rapped his fist on the worn desk. "Help me deal with Hellen. I have brains"—he pointed to himself, then swept his hand toward Ella—"finesse, and a little shade craft." He glanced at the door behind him, then turned back to Shane. "But I could use some muscle and some experience."

"That's about the nicest compliment you've ever given me, old man."

Jon chuffed, the wrinkles beside his eyes deepening. Though only forty-five, his time in prison showed in the shadow of his gaze and the swath of gray at his temples.

"You in?" Jon asked.

Shane raised his shoulders and threw out his arms. "Why not."

"Good." A subtle knock sounded at the back door. "Come in," Jon said.

The door swung open. A woman in blonde curls and black frills graced the doorway. For a second, Shane held his breath. He had been a little surprised to find Ella and Jon in Estbye, but this encounter had to be impossible. He swore under his breath.

A sultry smile grew on Illania Bradley's red lips. She rested her arm against the doorframe and popped her hip. "Well, well." She raked her vivid eyes up and down his form. "Miss me?"

"No," Shane said flatly. His entanglement with this rogue had come on the back of yet another life tragedy, and he'd sooner forget the whole affair.

Illania rolled her eyes and hummed in amusement.

Jon huffed and shook his head. His chair creaked as he leaned back. "Did you get a description from Mars?"

Fluffing her curls with her delicate hands, Illania said, "Our new friend, Miss Hellen, is accompanying the mayor at tonight's gala. She goes by Anette Brunner in affluent circles."

"Find her," Jon said. "All three of you. Find out if she's the top dog, or if we're really dealing with someone else."

Illania strode forward and looped her arms with Ella and Shane. "Come along, my friends. Neither of you look ready for a gala."

Shane groaned as she dragged him and Ella through the back door and into a large, dimly lit room. Cameron and Mars had gone. The low ceiling and peeling wallpaper gave the place a disheveled, claustrophobic atmosphere. A large table rested in the room's center, with fading sunrock sconces along the walls. An open door led to a small kitchen with another closed door beside it.

Illania guided Shane to a bench beside the table. She tugged at his coat. "Take it off."

He grumbled at her.

"Well," she said with a laugh, "don't take it *all* off. There is a child present."

"Gross!" Ella yelled as she headed into the kitchen.

Illania's humming laughter filled Shane's ears. He gritted his teeth. He'd fallen face-first for her charms once. This time he determined to keep his dignity. She leaned close as she pulled his coat from his shoulders. "What brings you to this fine establishment, Mr. zem'Arta?"

He scooted away from her and let his damp coat hit the floor. "I'm after a fugitive."

"Sounds fun." Illania ghosted a hand along the cut on his forearm. A chill ran through him. She peeled back his torn sleeve, revealing the open cut and the intricate black tattoos snaking his arm.

Ella returned and set a bowl of soapy water, a towel, and a medical bag on the table. She glanced at Shane and Illania, blushed deeply, and marched back to the kitchen, her brown curls bouncing as her hair tie came loose.

"Get into something fresh," Illania called after Ella. "You need to blend with the help."

"Right," Ella squeaked. A door creaked open and shut out of Shane's view.

Illania adjusted herself on the bench so that her thigh pressed against his. She clicked her tongue when he attempted to scoot away. She pressed the towel into the water bowl, then onto Shane's arm.

He grimaced from the sting. Illania kept a firm hold on him.

"How's my Remmy?" she asked.

"Fine," he said.

A smile tugged at her cheeks. "And my Zereen prince?"

Shane let out a long breath. "Illania," he said in a warning tone.

"I'm asking if you're okay, Shane. Friends want to know these things."

His breath caught. Friends? She had tried to kill him upon their first meeting. It had been a misunderstanding, leading to a falling out between her and Remm. Shane's most recent and regrettable tryst with her certainly did not boast friendship. Perhaps that's just how this woman operated.

"I'm fine," he said at last. He winced and bit his tongue as she strung a thick needle through his skin. The ointment she'd lathered on did little to dull the pain.

She worked with skill and speed, wrapping his forearm with a clean bandage to protect her work. Setting aside the scissors and extra cloths, she ran a hand up his arm. At first, the movement felt clinical. Then she trailed her fingers onto his chest. He caught her hand in a firm grip.

"We're not doing this," he said. "Not again."

Illania shrugged and stood. "I'll find you some dry clothes. You're a little taller than Jon, but his wardrobe should suit you fine. I have a special piece in mind from my own collection, too." She glided away from the table. A torrent of black shade smoke enveloped her into a trace. When she disappeared into the darkness, the shade's tendrils slipped past the inch-high crack under the door next to the kitchen. The chill in the air evaporated with her.

o— 6 —o

BAD COMPANY

Estbye, Taria
April 24, 1190 PT

Shane

Shane had only experienced highborn events as a bodyguard. He knew what to look for, the many tells of an ill-intended interloper. They either slipped in place before an event or after the lights went out. But they never came in the front door or drew attention to themselves.

"This is insane," he grumbled under his breath.

Across from him, Illania leaned forward on the carriage bench. Her low-cut pink dress, trimmed in ivory lace, would have made a harlot blush. She had more feathers in her hair than Shane thought reasonable, even for the noble-woman she impersonated.

Next to her, Ella chuckled while straightening her simple servant's coat and skirt. With her jacket open, the many throwing knives and tools glinted in the light of passing streetlamps. The carriage teetered as it rounded a turn. Through the coach window appeared the giant silhouette of the cathedral.

Illania moved closer to Shane, a braided metal collar in hand. "Put this on," she said, winking.

Flaring his nostrils, he glared at the indenture collar.

"It's not enchanted or anything," Illania said. "It won't choke you like the real ones if you run."

Shane flashed her a hard stare. "You sure?"

"Sweetheart," she said, "if I wanted to keep you to myself, I wouldn't need blood magic."

Sighing, he snatched the collar from her hand. He snapped it around his neck and sat back, folding his arms against his chest. His leather vest, riveted and stamped with Karthan symbols, squeaked as he shifted. A few sizes too small for him, the vest hung open, exposing the tattoos on his arms and chest.

Illania batted her eyes. "It suits you."

"I look like a . . ." Shane trailed off, not wanting to give her more reasons to tease him.

Illania and Ella giggled, bending forward.

"Why did you even have a thing like that?" Ella asked the rogue.

Illania flipped open her pink lace fan. "A woman never tells."

"Ugh," Shane grunted. "I'll need a bath after this."

A knock on the roof and the halting of the carriage brought his attention to the door.

"What happens when you can't charm your way in there?" he asked.

Flashing her brightly polished nails, Illania scooted toward the door. "When have my charms ever failed?"

The footman swung open the door and moved aside for Illania to exit. Shane followed, glad to escape the cramped coach but trepidatious about the task ahead.

Ella scurried past them toward the open doors of the cathedral, manned by several guards. A dozen gala guests mingled at the entrance, laughing and drinking. Ella whispered to a guard, who nodded and slipped into the building for a moment before returning with a servant. The servant carried a portfolio and perused the paper within as Ella spoke to him. He nodded, tapping the paper with his pen. Ella bowed low, imitating an outlander servant, and returned to Illania's side.

"We're in," Ella said.

"How?" Shane asked.

Illania snapped her fan shut. "I always put myself on the list of the best parties wherever I go. Just in case."

Shane sucked in a breath and shook his head. "In case you need to spy on someone? Rob them?"

Gathering her skirt, Illania stepped toward the door. "In case I feel like having a good time."

"Insane," Shane repeated in a whisper.

"Just play your part," she countered. "You're a disgraced Zereen with a crushing gambling debt. Indenture was the only option for you. You hate your lot in life. That shouldn't be too hard to pull off."

"Yeah," Shane grumbled, adjusting his collar. "I won't even have to act."

Illania swaggered ahead. "Exactly."

Immediately inside the doors, an antechamber crammed with guests greeted them. The crowd parted slightly for Illania and even more for Shane. Behind them, Ella shuffled through the throng.

A green-clad servant addressed Illania and bowed. "Lady Grallen. My master, Mayor Hofton, is pleased to welcome you as his personal guest."

Illania chuckled behind her fan. "I am most pleased to be welcomed."

The servant thrust his arm toward the open double doors leading from the antechamber into the grand hall. "Right this way."

Illania leaned toward Shane. "Come along, my pet. I must show you off to my friends." She fluttered her fan at Ella. "Miss Whitley, fetch me some red wine."

"Yes, mistress," Ella replied in a flat voice, then hurried off.

The servant called for the crowd to part and ushered Illania and Shane into the huge ballroom, once a sanctuary of worship. Judging by the risqué paintings and nude statues, the current owners had no qualms about bringing their baser appetites into a formerly sacred space.

A serving girl in a thin shift swaggered by with a silver tray of liberty cap mushrooms balanced in one hand. She stuck the tray under Illania's nose. "A fine evening awaits you, my lady."

Illania pushed the tray gently away with her folded fan. "My delicate constitution predisposes me to a lighter drug, I'm afraid."

The woman motioned to a side chamber, where puffs of blue and yellow smoke wafted across the threshold. "There is a pipe room."

Bowing her head, Illania said, "After I greet my host."

She glided through the crowd until she came to the edge of the polished marble dance floor, Shane on her heels. Half a dozen couples twirled about, in sync with the drums, spinet, and horns on the stage.

"Dead ahead. Gold dress," Illania whispered.

A portly, middle-aged man twirled a blonde woman wearing an extravagant golden gown. Her triumphant sneer soured her otherwise pretty face. Her eyes swept the room, and her cold smile grew. Across from Shane, a group of women fanned themselves while glaring at her.

Next to Shane, an elderly woman scoffed and muttered, "They let anyone into these parties of late."

The man on her other side, a face full of liver spots and wrinkles, cleared his throat. "I hear our dear mayor may have a proposal in mind for Miss Anette Brunner."

The old woman huffed. "He'd be spurning the Gothley family a second time."

Shane tensed when a cool, delicate hand slid down his bare arm.

"My, what a specimen you are!" said a brassy female voice behind him. She tugged on his false indenture collar as she slipped between him and Illania.

The rogue wore a neutral expression, but Shane caught the disapproving fire deep in her gaze as she bowed low. "Lady Monette," Illania said. "I'd heard you had taken up residence in this fine city. What a blessing for us all."

Monette, half a head shorter than Illania, nodded. "It pleases me to hear your approval. Forgive me, but I'm afraid I don't recognize you."

Illania curtsied. "Gretchen Grallen, my lady immortal. Daughter of Lord Farr Grallen of Rotira."

"Rotira," Monette said with a raised brow. "You're far from home."

"I enjoy traveling." Illania fluffed the blonde curls framing her cheeks. "At least until my father marries me off. I have no brothers, you know, so father's been particular. And Rotira is a difficult city to manage."

Monette gave an obligatory smile. "A rough place these last few decades."

Illania waved a gloved hand. "Oh, its reputation outstrips the reality. It's quite charming, especially in winter."

"Speaking of charming," Monette said, shifting her gaze to Shane. "Where did you manage to find this . . . fine beast."

A chill spread down Shane's back. His hands twitched with desire to wring the woman's neck. He forced himself to look away.

Illania linked arms with him. "Father insisted I have the most capable bodyguard."

Monette raised a brow. "Is that all?"

Illania winked, then giggled along with the immortal.

"Your wine, my lady," Ella said from behind them.

Illania turned and accepted the goblet. She stuck her nose into the cup and sniffed before taking a sip. Pulling the goblet away, she smacked her lips in appreciation. "Marvelous."

Monette hummed in agreement. "The vineyards of Estbye have no equal." She touched Illania's bare forearm and stepped closer. "Now, my dear, tell me where you're staying. You must come to the temple for the burning tomorrow."

"That would be lovely," Illania said. "I'm at the Creedmoor Manor on the south side."

"Come." Monette gestured toward the other end of the ballroom. "I'll introduce you to my new head priest." She swaggered through the crowd with Illania laughing at her side.

"Follow me," Ella whispered to Shane. She led him to the edge of the room where other bodyguards and servants loitered, ready to assist their respective noblemen and noblewomen at a moment's notice.

Ella leaned toward him as the music grew louder and faster. "Hellen is staying at the Hayden summer estate."

Shane grimaced. "If she's involved with the High Lord Warden, she's more than just an extortionist."

"My thoughts too," Ella said.

"Can we leave now?" he asked, tugging on the snug vest.

Ella glanced sidelong at him. "We have to play the full part. If we leave now, we'll seem suspicious. Besides, look at all the friends our lady mistress is making." She swept her hand toward the dance floor, where Illania and Monette flailed with a group of young noblewomen.

Shane endured two hours of watching the crowd of elites grow increasingly louder and more inebriated. One young man cried and rocked in a nearby corner. Hovering above him, a servant scolded his overuse of mushrooms.

When the music changed to an orchestral melody, the dancers bowed to one another and melded into the crowd. A dozen Drawlen priests carried candelabras onto the vacated dance floor. Monette entered, swaying and spinning alone among the candelabras. Her audience cheered when she performed a routine of spins and backflips, then shifted into the form of a great black raven and circled the room. She landed in her sapien form and bowed. The cheers increased.

The musicians transitioned to a lively tune as the priests removed the candelabras. The crowd wandered back to the dance floor.

Three times afterward, Monette sauntered toward Shane with lust in her eyes. At each attempt, Illania distracted her. By three in the morning, the crowd thinned as the musicians' melody softened. Monette stumbled in Shane's direction, licking her lips.

"Gretchen, darling," she called to Illania. "Might I borrow your man for a few hours?"

Shane clenched his jaw, glaring at Illania. The rogue opened her mouth but stepped back as a green-robed priest caught Monette's arm.

"My revered lady," he said. "Your carriage is ready."

Monette frowned. She gritted her teeth but smiled wickedly when Illania whispered in her ear.

"I'll hold you to that, Lady Grallen," she said.

"I am a woman of my word," Illania said, fanning herself and dropping into a curtsy. "Until then, good night, Lady Immortal."

"A good night to you as well," Monette said with a wave. She leaned heavily on the priest as he ushered her toward the front door.

Illania lingered with Shane and Ella until most of the guests had gone. "Let's go," she finally said.

As soon as Shane entered the carriage, he pried himself out of the leather vest and yanked a linen shirt over his head. He growled as he tore off the false indenture collar and glared at Illania.

"What did you tell her?" he demanded.

"I said she could have you in a few nights. Don't pout, zem'Arta. I got you out of a tricky spot. We'll all be gone before she misses you too much."

"You peddled me like a—"

"Now you understand how women feel. Relax. She was too drunk to remember most of this night anyway." Illania waved her fan. "Your dignity is spared."

The carriage pulled away, speeding down the open streets of Estbye. After a few blocks, it stopped in a secluded alley. Shane stepped out while the two women changed outfits. When they left the carriage, Illania, now clad in dark, loose trousers and a leather jacket, waved to the driver, who flicked the reigns and guided the carriage away.

She extended a hand to each of them. "Come, my lovelies. The real work begins."

Ella tightened her ragged brown coat around her smuggler's ensemble, a bulge or two indicating her stowed weaponry. She placed her hand on Illania's. They both looked expectantly at Shane.

"Bradley, if you're wrong about that immortal sprite," Shane said.

Illania rolled her eyes. "Then consider me indebted. Let's go."

Shane placed his hand on Illania's shoulder. The night squeezed in around them as the rogue initiated a trace.

Scenes of the city and countryside flashed across Shane's vision as Illania traced them mile by mile. They landed on the crest of a wooded hill overlooking the front lawn of a seaside manor.

Ella shivered next to Shane and crouched.

Illania studied the younger girl for a moment and placed a hand on her back. "We could manage without you, El, if it's too much."

"I'll be fine," she insisted.

Shane squatted next to Ella as a team of horses trotted ahead of a black carriage in the distance, guiding it along the gravel drive toward the house. Exiting the front door of the manor, two men approached the coach.

Though the darkness did little to hinder Shane's thurse eyesight, the far range made identifying the men difficult.

Illania bit her lip, closing her eyes as she sent a shade threading across the open space between the hill and the house. "Interesting. Your mole-faced friend appears to have found some fine accommodations."

"Kritcher?" Shane growled. He shifted forward.

Ella rose and pushed a hand against his chest. "You'll get yourself shot if you go after him now."

In the drive, Kritcher and his companion waved off the carriage, but no one had exited or entered it.

"Wonder what that was about," Illania said. "El, it looks like the carriage is being put away. Go take a look."

Ella nodded and entered the tree cover behind them.

When she had gone, Shane turned to Illania. "You could have sent a shade."

Illania drew in a breath, her face pinched in uncharacteristic concern. She gazed at the spot Ella had vacated. "You've had your share of hardships, zem'Arta." She turned soft eyes at him. "Think about the most horrible place you've ever been, where the most horrible things happened to you. Would you return willingly?"

Shane squinted at the shadow along the wood line. Visible only to his thurse eyes, Ella crept toward the carriage house. "It wouldn't be pleasant."

"We're in that place for Ella. When collectors went after Remm, when Ella was taken by Bruce Hayden's thugs. This—this is where she came."

A sour film formed on Shane's tongue. He swallowed and stared across the sprawling lawn toward the rocky beach two hundred yards away.

"Why did you bring her here?" he asked quietly.

"I gave her a choice," Illania said. "She refused to back down, said the job came first. It's the right choice, though she might not understand why. She must face this place, overcome the memory of what happened. She's come a long way from that frightened, broken girl. This is a necessary battle for her."

"You were with the rogues who rescued her?" Shane asked.

"I was."

"Why did you let Bruce Hayden live?"

"I didn't want to, Shane. I wanted so badly to strangle that man. Krishena forbade it. She said we came to save our friend, not to start a war. We left his mind broken though. Enough to shorten his life and his ability to rule. He will forever fear this place. He's not been back since."

"I don't think I could have left him alive," Shane said.

"A revenge killing would not have helped Ella. It would have made things worse. The temple would be out searching for anyone involved. This way, she's safe."

With their eyes fixed on the manor, they observed the interior of the grand dining room through brightly lit windows. Kritcher entered the room with his companion. He took a decanter from a buffet and poured two generous glasses.

Horse hooves on gravel clopped down the drive. A golden Drawlen carriage, hung with glittering sun crystals, rolled to the front door, followed by eight mounted graycoats. Kritcher and his companion again exited the manor.

When the driver opened the coach door, Monette, the fae immortal, stepped out hand in hand with a drunk and cackling Hellen, still in the guise of Anette Brunner. The human woman threw her arms around Kritcher's neck in a brief and clumsy embrace before stepping away. The immortal bowed her head as Kritcher and his companion dropped to their knees in reverence.

They rose and chatted for a moment, cackling all the while, though Shane couldn't understand their words. As they entered the house, the carriage headed toward the road. Some stable hands rounded the house and led away the military horses. Two Drawlen rangers entered the manor while another pair walked around back and the other four stationed themselves at the door.

Kritcher, Hellen, and Monette appeared inside the dining room, Kritcher again offering drinks. After spilling some of the liquor, he joined his companions in a toast.

Shane crawled forward.

Illania snapped out a hand, gripping his sleeve. "Joining the party?"

"Just getting a closer look," Shane said. "They're all drunk, and they'll be passed out in twenty minutes at this rate."

"We'd be burning idiots to tangle with eight rangers and an immortal," Illania insisted.

Shane paused and smirked at the rogue. He'd never once seen her cautious. "Calm down, Illy. Do you know what Monette's specialty is?"

"Um, no."

"She was an indenture in a circus troop—a dancer and an acrobat. She's Refsul's immortal bedmate. She might be handy with a knife and know how to pull a trigger, but she'd be no match for you."

Illania placed a hand on her hip. "Except the part where she can't die."

Raising a brow, Shane leaned close. "Aim to injure, not to kill. They only get a fresh start if they die. Otherwise, they bleed like anyone else."

○— **7** —○

TROUBLE

Estbye, Taria
April 25, 1190 PT

Shane

Shane extended and retracted his claws while watching Kritcher pace in the dining room, visible through the huge window. His heart raced as he contemplated options. Illania would be more than a match for Monette if she played her hand well. And she usually did.

He could handle the rest. They would both be impervious to Kritcher's mind craft, Shane due to his thurse heritage and training, Illania due to her nature as a ralenta. They would kill the soldiers and bystanders, disable Monette, and be off with Kritcher before the servants screamed for help. Shane could be out of this city, this territory, in a matter of days.

For once, Liiesh might even admit he did a decent job. Shane could put the outlands behind him and focus on more pleasant matters. Not that many pleasant matters occupied his life. He could invent some. Maybe he would take up a benign hobby in Palim. His father enjoyed woodworking. Perhaps he would visit and teach Shane some—

He blanched when Ella's stormy hazel eyes, framed by her pale face, interrupted his vision. She leaned into him, attempting to push him back toward the wood line. In his imaginative rapture, he had crept a few feet down the hill. The spell of his thoughts thoroughly broken, he dashed into the cover of the trees with Ella beside him.

"What the bloody burning fires were you doing?" she scolded in a whisper. "There are dogs down there."

"Dogs?" Illania darted next to them, blue eyes bulging. "My shade didn't spot any."

"They're in a silver-lined kennel around the other side of the house." Ella pointed to the path where she had scouted. "But they're not locked in. A trap for snooping ralenta."

Illania curled her lips into a silent snarl. "That's a little rich for a place the owner doesn't even visit."

"Bruce Hayden's sons have been using this manor as a hunting lodge the past year," Ella said.

Ruffling her brow, Illania said, "I thought he only had a daughter."

Ella shook her head as she glanced at the house. "He has a few bastard sons, but rumor is, he's fixing to legitimize them."

"I really should pay more attention to politics," Illania mused.

The light in the dining room extinguished, leaving only the reflection of the red Mortimus moon on the glass. Low beyond the churning sea, the two moons shone in the black sky, red dwarfing blue, the water sparkling like diamonds and rubies.

"You can lock the dog kennel," Shane said to Ella. "Illania and I can overtake Kritcher in the house."

"No," Ella said through gritted teeth. "This assignment is for information. We have it. Now it's time to leave. If you go for Kritcher now, you'll have collectors and purifiers on your tail all the way to Palim."

"Where did that black carriage go?" Illania asked.

Ella pointed to the carriage house across the lawn. "Kritcher has servants equipping it for smuggling. It appears he's planning to sidestep our operation and smuggle himself to Pelton. He might even hide behind Monette now that she's here."

Illania yawned and eyed Shane. "Why are you even after this Kritcher fellow?"

Shane sighed. "Let's say he robbed a bank."

"Let's say I don't believe you," she replied, fluffing her hair.

Shane cleared his throat, but Ella put a hand over his mouth and pointed. "Look," she commanded.

The steady clop of hooves met Shane's ears before a stable hand rounded the house with a saddled horse that stopped at the front door.

Kritcher's companion stepped out of the manor and mounted the stallion before cantering down the drive toward the highway. Shane fumed, his nostrils flaring. "This hunt needs to end."

"Relax, zem'Arta," Ella said. "You'll get your man."

"I've been chasing this burning fool for more than six weeks!"

Ella shifted her weight as she crouched. "Then you can wait a few more days."

Illania placed a hand on Shane's shoulder. "Patience has never been his talent." Before Shane could defend himself from her insult, she pulled them into a trace.

Shane, feeling thoroughly snubbed, returned with the two women to the smuggler's den as a band of gray light gathered in the east. With lips pursed and jaw twitching, Jon listened to their testimony about the gala and the Hayden manor.

He remained tensely quiet for a moment, then turned to Shane. "If you want Kritcher," he said finally, "you'll have to get him without my help. I don't tangle with Drawls."

"Papa," Ella protested. "We have to help him. You said you would."

"You've already told me Kritcher plans to smuggle himself out of Estbye," Jon said. "Don't expect to see him here again."

"Guess I'm done here, in that case," Shane said. He spun on his heels, intending to seek Daeven Kritcher on his own, as he'd originally planned.

Illania chuckled. "You're not really that shortsighted, Therman. Kritcher knows where you operate in this city. Whether he's ditching you or not, he's a liability. Either you're in this with zem'Arta, or you'll have to disappear."

Shane paused while grasping the door handle and turned. Ella's gaze flitted between Illania and Jon.

The smuggler closed his eyes and groaned. "Fires and moons," he muttered. He fixed on Shane. "This raises your price, Freelander. I don't normally take on this kind of risk."

Releasing his grip on the door, Shane remained pensive. Part of him wanted to spurn the renewed offer. But he knew how difficult this task would be without Jon's help. And he wasn't truly the one footing the bill in the end. "Name it. The spire lords have creditors, even here. I can get you just about any sum."

Jon narrowed his eyes. "Somulet Elixir," he said. "A full regimen of the real thing."

For a moment, Shane stifled a laugh. A rare and priceless medicine seemed a silly demand compared to Shane's offer of unlimited funds.

"That's expensive," Illania said.

"That's impossible," Ella groaned. "Papa, just ask for money."

"Somulet or nothing," Jon said firmly. "There's an apothecary in the central market who claims to have it. I assume you know what to look for."

Shane drew in a long breath through his nose. "Fine. Somulet."

"The real thing," Jon repeated.

"Yeah, I'll get you the real burning thing. First, I'm getting a nap."

Ella showed Shane to a cramped, musty spare room. The narrow bed creaked under his weight. Even the lumpy mattress and the mice scratching at the walls couldn't keep his exhaustion at bay.

When he woke two hours later, Illania presented him with his clothes, cleaned, dried, and stitched.

Cameron stood at the table in the great room, stowing a shiny pistol into her belt purse and throwing a loaded pack over her shoulder.

She turned to Jon. "See you in a few weeks, Jonny."

Leaning on the kitchen doorframe, Jon nodded. "Say hello to my wife and sons when you get to Lorinth."

"Always do," the woman said with a wrinkled smile. She shifted her gaze to Shane and winked. "Try not to drag this fool in too deep, lad. He can't help himself."

Shane hesitated. He was used to stern warnings meant in earnest, and to being disliked in general. But Jon ran with unusual folk. "I'll do my best," he said and tipped his head to Cameron.

She patted Jon's shoulder and left through the back hallway door.

Illania yawned and offered Shane her hand. "Come, my dear. Let's see if this drug slinger has the real thing."

Shane shoved his hands in his pockets. "Let's walk, Illy. I've had enough tracing for a while."

Twirling her hand in the air, the rogue batted her eye lashes. "Fine, fine."

She led him on foot to the apothecary about a mile away. The tidy storefront, tucked between a tea house and a tailor, boasted a tall window display of beakers and coiled tubes. Children pressed their noses to the glass, in awe of the rising, multicolored bubbles in the oddly shaped vials.

A crooked "open" sign dangled in the glass door. Leaving Illania out front, Shane stepped inside, a bell chattering above him as he crossed the threshold. Pungent, foreign smells assaulted his nose. The hum of a dozen pots bubbled in his ears. Shelves lined the walls, every inch occupied by neatly arranged tinctures, teas, and herbs.

"A moment," squawked a soprano voice from the back room. A spindly lady with dark eyes and raven hair emerged from the curtain covering the doorway. Her skin shone unnaturally white, and her ears, pointed and covered in gold earrings, protruded from her head. Her layered necklaces and scarves partially obscured her indenture collar.

She took one cursory look at Shane and hissed. "Ogre!" she yelled. "Be gone. I not serve your filth here. The master won't have it. Out!"

Shane sighed and put up his hands, backing out of the shop door.

"That was quick," Illania said, perched on a bench under a covered streetlamp.

Shane fixed her with a hard glare.

"Not keen on trolls?" the rogue asked.

"No."

Stretching her arms over her head, Illania stood and swaggered into the shop. Ten minutes passed, during which Shane sulked by the streetlamp, glaring occasionally at the children pressed to the display window. The littlest one, perhaps a girl of five, screeched at Shane and scampered off.

Illania emerged with a triumphant smile and a woven bag in hand. Shane reached for it. She clicked her tongue and snatched it behind her back. "First, tell me how wonderful I am."

"Illy," Shane warned.

"What was that?"

"You're . . . seriously?"

She inclined her head, taking a step back.

"You're wonderful," he said in a deadpan tone.

Illania swayed and smiled. "And beautiful."

He gritted his teeth. "And beautiful."

"Talented, clever—"

"Annoying," Shane said, cutting her off.

She sneered and handed him the bag. "You're no fun at all, Shane zem'Arta. That was a hundred and fifty tallies, by the way."

"Mother of . . ." Shane grumbled curses. "I'll have to spot you later. You walk around with that kind of coin?"

She fluttered her lashes. "I have an account with the merchant guild."

"You mean Gretchen Grallen has an account?"

Illania raised her shoulders and flitted her hands.

Shane peered into the bag. Blue liquid glowed inside a small vial. Unlike the imitation, in which sunrock particles would be floating, this liquid shone clear and free of bubbles. The real thing, indeed.

"Too bad this stuff isn't the miracle drug everyone claims it is," Illania mused.

"How would you know?" Shane asked as they walked along the street.

"Our master of poison has tried everything," she replied. "He swears the stuff is a myth. Wonder why Jon's so keen on it?"

"None of my business," Shane said. He plucked the vial from the bag and placed it in an inner pocket of his vest. While withdrawing his hand, the thin wedding band tumbled out from under his collar, dangling on the silver necklace. Hastily, he stuffed the treasure behind his shirt.

Illania stared at Shane's chest. Her usual smirk receded behind a sympathetic frown.

"Let's go," he said.

She remained still and met his gaze with surprising tenderness. "The dead are a heavy burden, Shane."

"You going all philosophical on me, Bradley?"

Illania crossed her arms. "So what if I am? You wear your hardships like armor, but they're really a poison."

"Do you ever mind your own business?" Shane crumpled the bag and tossed it toward a group of children playing a game.

Dodging a boy who darted to catch the bag, Illania laughed. "Once in a while, when a friend isn't in desperate need of unsolicited advice."

She squeaked in surprise when Shane yanked her into the alcove of the tailor's front door. As a black carriage raced by, she ceased her protest. The top half of the door hung open, giving Shane a view within. Hellen, the woman they'd spent all night spying on, leaned out the window, yelling something at the driver.

The driver was the same man who'd been with Kritcher at the Hayden manor. Six horsemen, all dressed in black, trotted after the carriage. As the carriage rounded a bend, Shane met Illania's narrowed eyes.

"Let's follow," Shane said, holding out his hand.

Illania placed her hand in his and traced, squeezing him into a world of breathless darkness.

Six times Hellen paused to direct a different rider to station himself at various points around the south harbor. Each time, she came closer and closer to Jon's smuggling den. Finally, her carriage halted at the dilapidated storefront.

"Are they policemen?" Shane asked.

Illania shook her head. "Worse. A rival smuggler. This is a takeover."

8

RIVALS

Estbye, Taria
April 25, 1190 PT

Jon

Jon held his breath, gazing at the plate before him. A half-raw egg soaked into burnt hashbrowns. The sausage, at least, looked edible. He smiled at his daughter. "Thank you."

"The stove went out before the eggs finished," Ella said from the kitchen door.

Jon nodded and forced a grin. A better excuse than usual. He speared the sausage on his fork but froze as the front doorbell chimed. A second later, a clattering erupted from the back hall. Without a word, Jon and Ella sprang from their places. He snatched a pistol from a kitchen cupboard while Ella stationed herself at the door to the back hall with another gun in hand.

Shattering glass tinkled in the storefront, followed by the creaking of the front door.

"We'll take them in here," Jon whispered. "No sense dying in a hallway."

Wide-eyed, Ella nodded.

Seconds dragged on, Jon's nerves confusing the breadth of time. Perhaps only half a minute passed before the front hallway door swung open, but time seemed frozen.

A burly man stepped through, gun sweeping the room. Jon spied through the crack behind the door, and Ella hid in the kitchen.

A second man entered the great room from the back hall. The two men nodded to each other. One of them spotted Jon but stilled when Ella appeared in the kitchen doorway and cocked the hammer of her gun.

"May we help you, gentlemen?" Jon asked as he stepped out from behind the door, his own pistol held ready.

"Are there more of you?" the first man asked, his voice unusually rough.

"Are there more of you?" Jon retorted.

The man whistled, and a woman wearing a dull-pink walking dress stepped through the front hall door. Her blonde hair, styled in twists upon her head, matched the paleness of her skin. Thin and short, she appeared no older than thirty.

"Hellen," Ella said.

The woman cocked her head. "I see my reputation has reached even this filthy corner."

"This is my home and place of business," Jon said.

Hellen threw her head back and laughed. "Not anymore, Mr. Taff. This, as they say, is a changing of the guards. Now, where can I find the Master Smuggler?"

Jon spat. "I'm afraid it doesn't work like that."

Hellen wagged a finger. "Perhaps not in the past. But things will be different starting today."

She stepped aside, and another woman entered. This one Jon recognized. Lithe and beautiful, Monette sauntered forward, unmoved by the four loaded guns occupying the space. Jon's blood pounded in his ears. He'd had one other encounter with an immortal. It had been tragic, dangerous, and had irrevocably altered his life.

Hellen bowed. "Welcome, my lady. Perhaps you can persuade these ruffians to cooperate."

The immortal smiled and smoothed her hands along her fitted silk dress. "Patience, my good servant. These are new pupils of mine. They must be handled gently." She turned to Jon, a play-acting smile on her pink face. "The Master Smuggler works for me now. I would very much like to make his acquaintance."

Two other armed men filed into the room from the front hall, crowding the space. Though they wore the shabby black uniforms matching the other men, these two carried themselves like soldiers.

"I will not ask again," Monette said.

Jon held his breath. Four guns against two. Hellen might be armed as well. And Monette had a reputation for being a decent fighter.

Round shots would not win this day, only his own cunning. He smiled and lowered his weapon. "You must have fallen further out of Lord Refsul's favor than I thought, Lady Monette. Attempting a takeover of Estbye's underground is a sad and desperate station for a Drawlen immortal."

Monette's eyes widened, her mouth agape.

Jon grinned. "Help me understand something. Is this little power play because of the purifiers who arrived in the city last night? Are you setting yourself up for a little war?"

Monette shifted her gaze to Hellen, then to her two accompanying guards. She gave a fake laugh, but her eyes shone brightly, and she trembled. "What lies you tell, Mr. Taff."

Jon cleared his throat. "Go and see for yourself. If I were you, I'd send one of these loyal servants here. Discreetly. If I'm a liar, you can chop my head off when you've found me out for sure. Otherwise . . ."

Monette raised her chin. "You're a bold man, Mr. Taff, attempting to hoodwink an immortal."

"This is no deception, ma'am," Jon said. "It's the simple truth. You fled to Estbye to avoid Refsul's temper. You've been appeasing him with your right hand and quietly undermining him with your left. He's found you out, and you've pissed him off for the last time. You figured you had a few months before he would send for you. You've been trying to set up a little underground empire so that you had somewhere to run when he did."

Snarling, Monette snapped her fingers. Two of the guards bowed and left through the front hall. The other two shifted uncomfortably. Hellen's hand twitched at her hip, where Jon felt certain a pistol resided in her pocket.

Ella's weapon remained trained on the man who'd first entered through the back door, her finger flat along the trigger guard.

Jon smiled, holstering his own weapon. "See. I knew you were one of the smart ones. Now, when your men return and tell you I'm right, you have some choices." He gestured to himself. "One, you can keep trying to strong-arm me, and it won't go well for you. Two, you can take advantage of my forgiving nature and pay the bill your crony here has racked up." He swung his hand toward Hellen. "Then get yourself on the next boat to Ostus before Refsul's agents know you're gone."

Behind Monette, beyond the reach of the sunrock sconces, a shadow deepened. For a second, the silhouette of a burly man and a slender woman appeared.

Jon glared at Monette. "You have a long life to live, Monette. You'll either be free with a little wound to your pride, or you'll be strapped to a cell wall in the Temple Setvan with your guts on display. I won't lose sleep in either case, so it will go better for you not to make an enemy out of the one man who can actually help you."

Monette barked. "What makes you think I need your help?"

Blackness descended on the room. Muffled cries mingled with a single gunshot. When the light returned, the two remaining thugs lay petrifying on the stone floor, one with his throat cut. Hellen squeaked and quivered in Shane's grip, his claws pressed into her throat and his other hand gripping her wrists.

Monette squawked, an ugly snarl on her face, the air shimmering around her. Before she could shapeshift, Illania traced behind her and knocked her across the back of the head with the butt of a dagger. The immortal fell unconscious into the rogue's arms.

"Good hit," Shane said, removing his claws from around Hellen's throat.

Illania winked. "Aim to injure, right?"

Jon held out his palm to Hellen. "Your bill is due."

Shane released Hellen's wrists. She shook her head, tears streaming from her eyes. "You must understand, Mr. Taff, I had no choice."

"My people have come to learn differently," Jon said, scowling. "But I won't waste time on the details. Pay my fee, plus interest, and I'll forget this little slip of integrity on your part."

Hellen put up her hands, nodding vigorously. "Fine. Fine. But you'll have to let me off to the bank."

"You can work that out with Mars later," Jon said. He turned to Illania. "Illy, tell Mars he can crawl out of his hole now."

Illania bowed with a flourish and said, "With pleasure," before disappearing into a swath of shadow.

Jon sighed, gazing at the mess of bodies in the room. "I'll take care of this lot. El, Shane, get Lady Monette on a boat."

Ella stowed her pistol and pointed to the immortal's unconscious form. "Mind picking her up, Shane?"

Shane balked. "You're not gonna help?"

"You're the one with all the muscles."

9

THE RAVEN LADY

Estbye, Taria
April 25, 1190 PT

Ella

With Shane carrying Monette's unconscious form, Ella led him down the back hall of the smuggler's den. They stumbled over the busted back door and bounded through the weedy garden. Entering the storage shed, Ella opened a large barrel meant for smuggling sunrock.

"Lay her in here," she said. "Be quick in case she wakes up."

Shane chuckled, displaying his fangs. Reaching into his vest pocket, he fetched a vial and uncorked it. He tipped the vessel of white liquid against Monette's mouth and opened her lips with his fingers.

"What's that?" Ella asked.

"Essence of Allunen," Shane said. "She'll sleep good and long with just a few drops."

Ella raised a brow. "Handy."

After Shane laid Monette into the barrel, Ella padded her back and legs with straw. She then placed a false bottom over the body and a shallow cask of whiskey above that. Securing the top, she and Shane hoisted the barrel onto a handcart. They exited the shed, Shane heaving the cart down the street. When they arrived on the wharf, the harbor bells tolled in the noon hour.

"Wait in the alley," she said to Shane. When he ruffled his brow, she added, "You gave every officer a run here yesterday. They might recognize you."

"What about you?" he asked.

She pointed to her fitted tan coat and green cap that hid her brown curls. "I'm perfectly forgettable in these parts."

Tugging at the cart, she dragged it along the uneven planks. After clearing the first rows of crates along the boardwalk, a frowning policeman halted her.

"You had that inspected?" he barked.

"On my way to the harbormaster," Ella said, bowing her head. The officer nodded and moved along, jutting his chin as though on important business.

Ella surveyed the dozen boats along the docks, spotting *Bethany's Hope*. Heaving and straining, she maneuvered the cart alongside the bulky galleon. Since Jon frequently hired this vessel for smuggling, he had a decent reputation with its captain.

"Ahoy, Captain," Ella yelled.

A stout man poked his head beyond the railing on the upper deck. "Ahoy, yourself. What's this?"

Ella pointed at the barrel. "A gift from Master Taff. If your destination is Ostus, that is."

"Well, Miss Taff, I do happen to be off that way soon."

"Then I have payment for the transport of this fine barrel."

"Payment, eh?" the man said, a greedy glint in his eye. "Let me come down there." For a moment, he disappeared, then bounded down the gangplank to meet her. He whistled to his crewmen. "Hoist this up," he commanded.

Two men on the docks scrambled to roll the handcart up the plank, returning it, minus the barrel, a few minutes later.

Ella handed the captain a purse of coins. "Don't count it now," she whispered.

"Shall I not look in the barrel either?"

"You will, soon enough."

"When's that?" the captain asked.

"When you can't stand not to." She patted him on the shoulder. "Fine sailing, Captain."

He chuckled and backed toward the gangplank. "And a fine day to you, miss."

Ella guided the empty handcart down the side street to where Shane waited. Behind them, *Bethany's Hope* floated away from the docks. They headed back to the smuggler's den, walking the first block in silence. The Drawlen temple bobbed in and out of view as they weaved through the streets.

Ella bit her lip but couldn't contain her burning question. "Is she really immortal? I mean, isn't it just their ploy?"

Shane sighed. Down the wide street, the temple, glistening gold and pale pink in the noon sun, hovered above the low tenements. "There are a lot of frauds who claim it. But Monette is the real thing, unfortunately for her."

"How do you know?" Ella asked.

He grunted, shadows clouding his expression.

She stared at the temple ahead and the spires of the Creedan cathedral jutting above the rooftops a few blocks away. "Well, I think it's all a crock."

Kicking a pile of pebbles in the road, Shane chuffed. "You're not alone. Either way, they have your country under their thumb."

Her face scrunched. "As opposed to your mind-reading fliers? Is it true that terrion can twist a man's mind so far, he breaks?"

Shane stiffened. "One hundred percent."

"All of them?"

"Only the powerful ones, the mind renders."

Ella wrinkled her brow, standing still even as Shane moved ahead. "I've always wondered—"

She stilled when Shane placed a firm hand on her shoulder. She followed his narrowed gaze and waited.

After a few seconds, two men dressed in shimmering silver robes and sporting shaved heads marched past—Drawlen purifiers. They were the death dealers of the temple, those who came after questions had been answered, after guilt had been decided. The crowd parted for them like insects fleeing a grassfire. Once they reached the boardwalk, they headed toward the harbormaster's office.

Ella let out a long breath, curling her trembling hands into fists.

Shane watched the people mingle back together after the purifiers strode out of sight. "Your old man wasn't bluffing."

Ella shook her head. "Monette's been sinking her claws into the neighborhood gangs the past few months. It was only a matter of time before she targeted bigger operations like ours. I just didn't think she'd be bold enough to come to us herself."

When he cast his crystal-blue eyes on her, they changed to a darker shade. "You need to get out of Estbye, Therman," he said. "Purifiers won't leave any rocks unturned."

"What about your bank robber?"

Shane's lips twisted into a smirk. "Maybe we can give him a ride."

They returned to the smuggler's den to find the back door already repaired and the great room clear of bodies. Even the bloodstain had been scrubbed away.

Jon and Mars Quinley sat at the table, pouring over their doctored supply logs. Shane interjected when Ella opened her mouth to make her report.

"You've got a problem, Therman."

"Monette?" Jon asked.

"No," Ella said, pushing Shane aside. "She got on her way just fine. But purifiers are looking for her. They arrived at the docks just after we put her on a ship."

"You should clear out of here," Shane said. "Now."

Jon pursed his lips, glancing between a quivering Mars and Shane standing casually at the kitchen door as though this were a normal spring morning.

"It was bound to be a problem," Jon said finally. "Even without Monette's involvement, Hellen was trouble enough. I'm keeping her in the cellar until we can sort all this out." He turned to Mars. "You'll have to clear the warehouse. I'll take care of the den."

A warm giggle tickled Ella's ear a second before Illania appeared at her side. She draped an arm around Shane's shoulder, scooting closer as he attempted to step away.

"Don't leave, my dear," she said. "I have news for you."

He glared at her.

"Your prize is trying to run off."

"Kritcher?"

Illania twirled a lock of blonde hair around her finger. "Unless you have another pet fugitive I don't know about. Those two men Monette sent out took one look at the purifiers and ran with their tails tucked. I don't think we'll see them again. But Kritcher is ripe for picking."

Shane turned his attention to Jon, who nodded.

"Secure your man, Shane," he said. "We'll be ready to get you out of Estbye today." To Ella, he added, "Get a cart prepared."

She nodded, the thrill of another job thrumming in her bones.

Illania offered her hand to Shane, who took it with a grimace. They vanished in a torrent of darkness.

o— 10 —o

THE ESTATE

Estbye, Taria
April 25, 1190 PT

Shane

By early afternoon, Shane and Illania materialized on the hill overlooking the Hayden estate. Dark, angry clouds assaulted the sky from the western horizon.

At the front door of the manor, a black carriage waited. The driver, a man in a dull-blue suit, scrambled around the carriage. He checked the tethers on the two horses and inspected the cab.

Kritcher emerged from the manor's entrance with a suitcase in hand. He placed it in the driver's awaiting arms while barking orders at him.

"The upstairs window," Illania said. "Look."

Shane's gaze shifted upward. He caught sight of a man in the window who appeared identical to the man in the driveway yelling at the servant.

"Fires," Shane muttered.

Illania flicked her hand and shut her eyes. "We need a closer look."

The chill of a shade swept by Shane's face. A gray shadow hovered above the grass, speeding down the hill. It weaved through the bushes alongside the house, creeping toward the men in the driveway.

After a few seconds, Illania opened her eyes. "I'd bet my life the man in the carriage is the decoy."

"I believe you," Shane said as the carriage lurched forward. The horses heaved into a steady trot, and the carriage rounded a tree-lined bend in the road.

The man in the upstairs window waited momentarily, gave a satisfied nod, and disappeared.

With a mischievous smirk, Illania nudged Shane. "Shall we dance?"

Without reservation, Shane put his hand in hers. The world winked out, then solidified around him in the form of a hall decorated with framed paintings and bordered by sweeping archways. Floral wallpaper peeked out from behind the portraits, most of them depicting pale men in frilly suits and wearing gaudy rapiers. The dark veil of Illania's shade kept her and Shane invisible.

"Where is Mr. Herold?" a woman's voice asked from far down the hall.

"The basement," an unfamiliar man answered in a hushed tone.

"I don't know what the master is thinking, taking in all these strange folk."

The man grumbled as he approached, "Keep your voice down."

The two people—servants, judging by their attire—passed by without a glance and hurried off in different directions.

"Where do you suppose the basement stairs are? I can't remember," Illania asked in a hushed tone.

Shane shrugged. He stayed tight behind her as she crept down the hall. All the while, the shade cloaked them, casting the world in pale shadow and muffling the sounds of the house.

They opened a few doors, finding only closets or drawing rooms. Finally, they discovered a narrow door near the kitchen leading to a downward staircase. Two ornate sunrock sconces lit the stairwell and the landing below. Illania closed the door behind them, using a shade to muffle the creak of hinges.

A low-ceilinged hallway led off the landing. The basement boasted the same care and detail as the main floor.

Illania stopped and shut her eyes. She smirked when her shade snaked along the ground, returning from its scouting mission.

"Found him," she said. "In the study just ahead."

They stopped at an open door leading into a cramped office. Kritcher sat at a desk facing the far wall.

Shane charged forward, Illania on his heels. A wire snagged Shane's foot, causing him to stumble. A creaking hiss, followed by the whine of hinges, proceeded the snapping of the cord at his feet.

He caught himself on the back of the chair, jostling the man who flopped limply onto the floor. Shane gaped at the blank face of the mannequin he'd taken as Kritcher, just as the door slammed. The lamp on the desk teetered and fell, the cheap sunrock dust within spilling onto the floor in a smattering of dull blue. It pulsed for a moment, then faded out.

"What in the fires?" Illania yelled. "I can't trace. I can't see a damned thing!"

Shane slowly adjusted to the lightless room. Even his sharp eyes struggled to identify any details. What he could make out caused him to shudder. The artwork on the wall was not hung but painted onto the plaster surface. The texture of the walls, which he had taken for wallpaper, turned out to be a mesh lining covering the walls, ceiling, and floor.

"The room's lined with silver," he said in a bitter tone. "A burning trap." Howling and seething, he threw himself at the door with his full strength. It quivered but remained unyielding.

"Oh, you won't get out of here, ogre," came Daeven Kritcher's voice from beyond the door. "This is a special room made for Bruce Hayden's—shall we say, guests. The Drawlen collectors will find you quite comfortable in there when they arrive in a few hours."

"You little fiend!" Shane growled and pounded the door.

Kritcher cackled triumphantly, a sound that faded with his retreating footfalls.

Illania pressed her back to the wall and slid to the floor, head in her hands.

Shane continued thrusting his shoulder against the door. Each vibration mocked him like Kritcher's laughter, leaving him all the more enraged.

Illania got up and paced the room. "You're wasting your strength."

He slumped into the chair and kicked the mannequin across the room. Even the papers and baubles on the desk were fake—merely painted wood.

She placed a gentle hand on his shoulder. "I'm sorry, Shane. This is my fault."

He shook his head. "I fell for it, too."

He stood and stepped to the side, his foot rolling on the wire he'd blundered into upon entering the room. He kicked it, muttering a string of Karthan curses under his breath. Twice in two weeks, he'd fallen for the same damn trick.

Gritting her teeth, Illania stared in the direction of the door. "The second they open that door, I'm tracing us out of here. We'll be fine. We'll be perfectly fine."

Ella

On the seaside highway, near the turn to the Hayden estate, Ella jumped from the hay wagon. She nodded to the farmer, whom she'd already paid to transport her out of his way. He returned the gesture and continued down the road.

The rain, which had been torrential all afternoon, now fell softly on the road and the landscape to the east. The sun, hugging the western horizon, frosted the fleeting clouds in ribbons of red, purple, and gold.

Ella struggled through the tall hedges marking the border of the Hayden estate. She slunk along them for a hundred yards before entering the wood line and ascending the hill beside the house. No one stirred from what she could see through the manor windows or the carriage house.

She fought the trembling in her bones that betrayed her fear, both for being in this horrible place again, and for knowing her friends had not returned.

The sun set, night sweeping the land from the east like a dark blanket slowly drawn across a bed. Around her, the crickets and night critters struck up their chorus. Only a few lamps glowed in the quiet house.

As Ella surveyed the front entrance, the door swung open, and Kritcher marched onto the drive with the same companion from the night before. They strode toward the carriage house.

She slid silently down the grass-covered hill and pressed herself against the stonework of the house, beyond view of the two men. She edged along the bordering barberry bushes, her thick canvas coat protecting her from the thorns.

Arriving at the front stoop, she climbed the stone banister and scampered across the stairs. Then she vaulted over the opposite banister and landed with a soft thud on the far side of the front entrance.

Tiptoeing to the corner, she waited for Kritcher and his accomplice to stride into the horse barn behind the carriage house. The estate now bathed in darkness, the dogs remained her only obstacle.

She crept toward them. The kennel looked like a benign shed, though the shepherd dogs grunted and panted within. Although the door appeared closed, Ella knew from her earlier inspection that a section of it could swing up for the dogs to roam.

Deftly, she flipped the outer latch securing the dog door. This, at least, would give her time if the dogs got wind of her later. She crept toward the stable. Placing herself in the shadows beside the door, she listened.

"We'll split the bounty for the ralenta," came Kritcher's voice. He sounded snide and pompous, not at all like the desperate man peddling his false plight as he'd done the previous day in Jon's office.

"And the Freelander?" the other man asked.

Kritcher chuckled. "An ogre would fetch us something."

"Are you sure I should go to the temple? What about Hellen?"

"We'll see to Hellen," Kritcher said.

Two other male voices chuckled.

Kritcher grunted. "She was paying a visit to that bottom-feeding smuggler. If he's done something rash, I'll put a round shot in him. But we're not equipped to move a ralenta, and I know that troll can put up a fight. The collectors will have to come here themselves."

A horse whinnied, and Kritcher trotted out of the barn on horseback with the other man following on a dappled mare. After him came two mounted men dressed in black uniforms like the ones who had accompanied Hellen and Monette to the smuggler's den.

Sweat beaded on Ella's face despite the cold. The house loomed. Shane and Illania were trapped inside. And Ella knew exactly where. It was like being trapped in that room again. Her chest squeezed. Her heart felt as though it would rupture from the sheer memory. She sank to the dew-covered ground.

Forcing herself to breathe slowly, she recalled her mother's words: *You are not your tragedies, child. They do not own you. You must overcome. Turn your hardships into triumphs.*

Time stopped. Slowly, as if lifting an immense weight, she crawled forward. She rose to her knees, then to her feet. One foot before the other, repeat. She passed the dog kennel. She reached the house.

"I am not the prey," she whispered so quietly she barely heard her own words. "I am the vindicator. I am the predator's predator."

Slipping through the kitchen door, she entered an empty room. Footsteps approached from the hall. Ella ducked below the worktable. Through the pots stored on the lower shelf, she saw a skirt swishing closer. As the woman's boots clomped across the stone floor, Ella slid to the far end of the table and behind a post.

When the servant woman busied herself at the sink, clanking dishes and sloshing water, Ella fled from the room. This brought her to the very door she sought. She fished an oil tube from an inner coat pocket and popped the cork. With the hinges sufficiently greased, the door opened silently.

Each downward step sucked the air from her lungs. Every glint from the gold-flecked wallpaper, which was burned into her memory, brought the sensation of slimy ropes winding around her whole body.

With shaking knees, she stood before that horrible door. Bruce Hayden's face—wrinkled, smiling—played, unwelcome in her mind. He reached for her.

"I'm here," she called out.

"Ella?" came Illania's voice from the room.

"It's me," Ella said. "I'll get you out. Just give me a minute."

"You'll need a key," Shane said. "That's a Yvean compound lock."

Ella smiled as she fetched her lock picks from a pocket in her cuff. "A minute is all."

She knelt before the lock. It became the only thing she saw. The only thing in the world. The filthy sensation on her skin dissipated. Her breath returned, deep and even. Bruce Hayden fled from her mind. Only the lock existed and her power to open it.

Pop. She swung open the door.

Footsteps and shouts came from the stairs. Illania flew over the threshold as a shadow rushed past Ella. The footsteps became a heavy body tumbling down, down, down. A man in a tailored servant's coat lay on the floor at Illania's feet. His eyes stared blankly at the ceiling, his skin turning gray with petrification. Soon, he would become stiff as stone. Perhaps someone would find him and burn his body. If not, in about three days, a shade would rise from him like steam from a lake on a cold morning, and he would rot.

Ella turned away. "You didn't have to kill him, Illy."

Illania snarled. "I'm a rogue, not a saint. And this one had it coming. You should have heard how he talked about me earlier."

Shane emerged from the room, which Ella avoided entering. "All right, ladies. Let's get our guy and ditch this city."

Illania put a frigid hand on both of their shoulders. She pulled them into a trace just as a woman screamed from the top of the stairs.

11

DEMANDS

Estbye, Taria
April 25, 1190 PT

Jon

Jon shut the tailgate on the smuggling cart. With the back of his sleeve, he wiped his sweating brow, then gave the storage shed a cursory inspection to make sure he'd packed everything. Too bad about the drama of the last two days. This really had been one of his best setups. For the last nine months, the den had served his smuggling network well.

Since leaving Langry prison almost a year ago, this had been a place of healing and comfort. Some wounds, the metaphysical kind, would never truly heal for him. But he called the open world home now, and he'd built a name for himself, even if it was a pseudonym. The Master Smuggler was no longer a hoped-for title, but a respected and mysterious figure known throughout the Corigish commonwealth.

He nodded and smiled at the tidy cart. He would make a new start in another den. There were plenty of neglected corners in this city. At least this time, he didn't have to evacuate his whole family. Domestic life in Lorinth had its advantages, even if his wife was there by legal order.

He stepped out into the garden and shut the shed door behind him. Night had fully bloomed. He entered the den through the back door and walked down the hall.

"I'm ready for the wood ox, Mars," he called out while approaching the entrance to the great room.

When Jon crossed the threshold, Mars greeted him in silence with wide eyes and trembling hands. Kritcher stood beside him with a cocked pistol pointed at his temple. Flanking the pair were two men dressed like the bodyguards who'd come that morning with Hellen and Monette.

One of them pointed his gun at Jon. With a sigh, Jon put up his hands.

"So nice to have your cooperation," Kritcher said. "Where is my dear Hellen?"

"The basement." Jon grinned, pointing to the door. "Taking a nap." Even with a gun pointed at him, he couldn't resist a joke. Hellen had screamed herself hoarse before Jon managed to get a sleeping draught into her.

Kritcher beamed like a man drunk on his own good luck. "We'll see to her soon enough. In the meantime, you'll be interested to know that your friends have also found themselves taking a break in another basement. They're about to be picked up by Drawlen collectors. I'm sure the Black Veil order would be keen to know you harbor an unregistered ralenta and a Freelander troll."

"I'm sure they would." Jon dropped his hands to his side. "But I feel like there's a second option you're about to offer me."

Kritcher chuckled. "Why do you say that?"

Jon shrugged. "You would have shot us both already."

"True enough." Kritcher trained his gun off Mars. "As it happens, you have something I want."

"Which is?"

"The identity of the Master Smuggler. That and fifty thousand tallies will put a key in your hand and my men off your back. You can go to the Hayden estate and set your companions free. If you move quickly, you may beat the collectors."

Jon barked in laughter. "With that much money, you don't need the Master Smuggler, Mr. Kritcher."

Kritcher's mouth twitched into a snarl, probably at hearing his real name. "Many interested parties would pay good sums to know his name and face. Knowledge is power, as they say."

"I'm afraid I'll have to decline your offer."

"Not even to save your dear friends?"

A chill rose in Jon's spine. He smiled in earnest. "The type of companions I have rarely need saving."

Kritcher cackled. His eyes turned fully black, locking Jon in their strange power. "In this case, I think you'll find—"

Just like that morning, shade-induced darkness descended on the room. It broke the strange spell Kritcher had cast upon Jon, giving him a blistering headache. The sound of splintering wood mixed with Kritcher's yelp. When the light of the sunrock sconces returned, Illania straddled the petrifying form of one of Kritcher's guards. The other had vanished, probably through the front hall where the door hung on one hinge. Mars cowered under the table with his hands over his head.

Kritcher swung his gun toward Jon, his eyes bulging. But Shane shoved Jon out of the way and stared Kritcher down with a wolfish smile. Kritcher's mouth gaped when Ella flew across the room. Her leg outstretched, she kicked him in the face, knocking him unconscious, his head slamming into the table. He slumped on the ground, the gun clattering beside him.

"Damn it, Mouse!" Shane yelled. "You spoiled my moment!"

Ella recoiled at his scolding. "Sorry, I was trying to be efficient."

"There's another guard," Jon said, pointing toward the broken door.

Illania bowed and waved her hand before disappearing in a trace.

Inspecting the guard on the floor, Shane ripped open his black coat. A gray shirt lay beneath it, the uniform of a Drawlen ranger.

"Burning Drawls," he growled.

"It's time to go," Jon said to Mars.

The thin man crawled out from his hiding place and rubbed his quaking hands together.

Jon signaled to his daughter. "You and Shane get the cart ready. The wood ox is in the barn at the end of the block.

"Where are we going?" Ella asked.

"Home."

Ella thrust a hand toward Mars. "What about him? What about the job? Isn't Hellen still in the basement?"

Jon patted Mars on the shoulder. The man shivered.

"Mars will see to that," Jon said. "We need to get Kritcher out of town, and not on the road to Pelton. It's the first place his friends will look."

Shane rolled Kritcher onto his back and fished through his pockets. "As long as I get him back to Palim, I'm willing to take a few detours."

"You got my payment?" Jon asked.

Shane leaned back and patted his vest pocket, offering Jon a fanged grin.

Jon nodded. "Good."

Illania sauntered through the front hall doorway, re-pinning a fallen curl. "That was some much-needed exercise."

"You'll have more," Jon said. He pointed at the dead graycoat. "See that this fellow is found well away from here."

Illania wrinkled her nose. "I dropped the other one in the canal."

"That suits me fine," Jon said.

She stretched her neck, eyeing Jon and the others. "Are you leaving town?"

"Yes." Jon pointed his thumb at Ella and Shane. "And these two trouble-makers are coming with me."

Illania gave a wide smile and bowed. "Well, I'm happy to stay and clean up the riffraff. I'll need to head back to Rotira soon though."

Jon crossed his arms. Exhaustion set in like a sudden wind. He blinked, willing his fatigue away. "I appreciate your commitment to being thorough. See you another time, Bradley."

Illania scooped Ella into a sisterly hug. "You're my little hero, you know."

Ella blushed deeply. "Thanks. See you, Illy."

Illania released her and extended a hand to Shane. "When you get back to the Freelands, try to keep my Remmy out of too much trouble."

Shane squinted at her. Then, he grinned and gripped her forearm, giving it a firm shake. "That's a tall order. No promises."

12

THE RED WOLF

The western countryside of Taria
April 26, 1190 PT

Shane

Shane hopped off the driver's bench of the covered cart and rubbed his back, wincing. After sitting more than six hours, it spasmed from the sudden movement. His boots squelched in the cold mud as he approached a tangled clump of vines blocking their trail. Jon and the wood ox pulling the cart grunted in unison. Shane grasped the vines and cleared them away from the fence. Lifting the rusty latch on the gate, he swung it open.

When the cart passed through, he re-latched the gate. A steady rain started, cold droplets pelting them from a darkening sky. Gripping the frayed rope at his feet, Shane replaced the tangle of brambles that disguised the trail to the smuggler's cabin.

He vaulted over the fence, trotted along the rolling cart, and swung himself into place on the driver's bench. Jon offered a perfunctory nod.

"You keep a cool head," he said through the tobacco pipe stuck in his teeth. "I really thought that highway captain was going to put up a fuss about us leaving town so early."

Shane rolled his shoulders. "He was just grumpy."

Around a bend, a quaint log cabin appeared. Apart from the black tar paint covering the logs, it could have been any hunting shack in the Freelands. Across the clearing stood a barn just big enough to hold the cart and the wood ox.

Jon steered toward the barn. When he came to a stop before the wide, latched door, he whistled.

Ella moaned from within the cover of the cart. She poked her head through the front flap, blinking away fatigue.

"Get the cabin ready," Jon said.

Ella nodded and yawned. She trudged through the mud and tall grass toward the cabin.

Shane opened the barn door. Jon flicked the reigns, sending the wood ox heaving forward. The creature dipped its head low, its horns inches from scraping the ground. It mewled happily as Jon and Shane unbridled it and led it to a pile of hay.

They pushed aside the barrels and crates filling the cart and opened the false floor, exposing Kritcher's unconscious form in the smuggling compartment.

With one heave, Shane extracted the man from the cart and shoved him into a sitting position against a post. Kritcher grunted groggily, his head bobbing from side to side.

"Need anything?" Jon asked.

"I'll be fine," Shane said. "Get to the cabin with El. This fool has a little flier in him. Maybe not enough to snap your mind, but enough to give you a headache."

Jon put up his hands as though to say, "no thanks," and stalked off, shutting the barn door behind him.

With a thick rope, Shane secured Kritcher to the post, tightening the final knot just as the man groaned into waking.

"Evening, whelp," Shane said.

Kritcher moaned and blinked, his mud-brown eyes struggling to focus.

Shane slapped his cheeks lightly, receiving a hiss. "I've been waiting a long time to have this chat," Shane said. "I'm out of patience."

"You're quite sly for an ogre," Kritcher slurred, glaring and clenching his teeth.

Shane snorted. "You're quite cheeky for a doomed man."

A haughty smirk alighted on Kritcher's face. "You must really be a fool. Do you think the Spire Watch will accept anything from you, a thrice-marked?" He stared at the scars on Shane's face. "Even if I were a prize for the First Lord himself, they would no sooner allow the likes of you in their courts. You may have found plentiful pastures in the outlands as a bounty hunter, but the homeland has no place for you, convict."

"But you are a prize for the First Lord," Shane said. "So much that he won't mind receiving you from a marked man. Or did you think I was after you for the bank fraud?"

Kritcher blanched. His face twitched into a false smile. "What other grievances have you imagined of me?"

Shane grabbed a bench and straddled it, leaning forward. "Let's start with you stealing the deed of Vernon vel'Tamar's house."

"That—what?" Kritcher barked. "Besides the fact I am innocent, how does supposedly defrauding a silk trader make me a prize for Lord Romanus?"

Shane leaned back and scratched the scruff of his neck. He needed to shave again. "For a man who put up such a long con, you certainly missed some important details. Mr. vel'Tamar is not a silk trader. He's an agent of the First Lord."

Kritcher's face contorted. He appeared on the edge of laughter. When Shane's face remained serious, Kritcher quivered. He dropped his façade of innocence.

The air of early night turned ice-cold, a static sensation running up Shane's arms. Mind craft. He smiled.

"There are advantages to being an ogre," he said. "Your little magic tricks won't work on me."

The spike of mind craft peaked for a second, and Shane tasted Kritcher's full power. He had to be at least a quarter terrion to have that level of craft. If the circumstances had been different, he might have qualified as a mind render. Shane laughed at the attempt.

Kritcher recoiled. "I demand a fair trial. It's my right as a Freelander."

Shane reared back, scowling. "State your case, fool."

"I demand a judge."

"I *am* your judge," Shane said. "And your jury. And your executioner."

Kritcher's face twisted into an ugly, evil sneer. "You're marked, filth. Maybe they give you credence out here, but in Palim—"

Shane growled under his breath. He had grown tired of this pompous, malevolent man. He reached into his vest pocket and retrieved a black parchment. A gold wax seal decorated the folded paper, the impression of a sun silhouetting a crescent moon stamped into it.

Kritcher licked his lips, his face growing white. "You're not a bounty hunter."

"No."

Kritcher stared with a slack jaw. His chin quivered. "You're him," he whispered. "You're—I thought the Red Wolf was a rumor, a scare tactic."

Shane shrugged. "Started that way. But the name stuck." He retrieved the vial of sleeping elixir from his pocket. "I hereby arrest you in the name of the

Red Watch, under the authority of the First Lord, for conspiracy to blackmail an agent of the state, and for treason against the Freeland coalition."

Trembling, Kritcher thrashed against his bindings. "I can name—I have—"

Shane popped the cork on the vial. "I'm sure you have all kinds of things to tell me. But we'll save it for someone who cares."

"Who?" Kritcher demanded.

"You nearly conned a Red Watch commander. You've earned yourself a seat at the big kids' table."

"Not the First Lord. Please."

"You'd rather talk to his brother?"

"No. Neither. The arbiters—"

Shane barked with laughter. "Don't handle matters of national security. You played a bad hand, Mr. Kritcher. Your debt is due." He towered over the man and forced enough potion down his throat to keep him asleep for days.

Kritcher fought and wiggled. After a long, desperate whine, he fell unconscious. Shane heaved him back into the smuggling compartment just as Jon entered the barn.

"Get some rest, zem'Arta," Jon said. "I'll keep watch."

Shane patted Jon on the back as he left. When he entered the single-room cabin, he tossed his coat atop a chair by the small table.

Ella slouched on the couch next to the warmth of the heat stones. She leaned forward and turned the stones in the hearth with a pair of iron tongs. After replacing the tongs on a hook, she settled back onto the couch, which creaked as Shane settled next to her.

Silence accompanied them. From her coat pocket, Ella fished a mess of papers and handed them to Shane. He unfolded one of them, revealing the wanted poster she'd filched the other day.

"Damn," Shane said with a smile. "Remm was a funny-looking kid."

Ella smirked. "Tell him to write once in a while."

Shane traced the words on the poster. "Not even sure that whelp can read."

Giggling, Ella nudged his shoulder.

Shane settled back and stuffed the papers into his vest pocket. He tapped his foot to break the quiet that followed. He thought of all they'd been through in the last two days, what Ella had overcome to see them safely here. His tapping stopped. "I'm sorry you had to go back there," he said. "The house. . ."

Ella fluttered her lips. "We all face our ghosts sometime. I didn't want an old tragedy to create a new one."

Gulping, Shane gazed into the glowing heat stones in the hearth. Ella squeezed his shoulder as she rose, then climbed into the loft. The creak of a bed preceded her even breathing.

Sitting alone, Shane fished out Nola's wedding band, still secure on the delicate silver chain around his neck. He stared at it. Illania's words hounded him: *"You wear your hardships like armor, but they're really a poison."*

The heat of the hearth stones radiated. They were smith-grade rocks, capable of melting metal. Perhaps he should. . .

His fingers trembled. He imagined the ring softening and dripping among the stones. Quivering, he banished the vision and curled his fist around the wedding band. "Stay with me just a little longer," he whispered.

ABOUT THE AUTHORS

K. R. Solberg and C. R. Jacobson are the daughter-mother writing team behind the fantasy series, The Palimar Saga. Together, they write gripping stories and argue about homophones.

K R Solberg believes in the enduring power of story. A wordsmith and graphic artist, she dwells in the woods of Wisconsin with her patient husband and their two book-obsessed children. She is disastrously introverted and chronically sarcastic. Her storytelling journey began under the nurturing wing of her mother and co-author. Her father's dramatic bed-time readings of Tolkien contributed to this obsession.

C. R. Jacobson, a retired English professor with 41 years of teaching, now channels her expertise into crafting captivating stories. With a meticulous eye for detail, she weaves narratives rich in depth and authenticity. The Palimar Saga reflects her love for storytelling and family. She's a small-town Minnesota soul who now calls the sun and sands of southern Florida home with her husband and enjoys tending her garden, experimenting with recipes, brewing kombucha, and spoiling her 11 grandchildren.

This story began as a creative effort between mother and daughter when K. R. was a high school sophomore. As a free-spirited, flighty, and quietly rebellious teenager, she didn't seem to have much in common with her steady, disciplined, hard-working mother. Nothing mends a strained relationship like working together toward a unified vision. At its core, *The Palimar Saga* tells the story of one family as they strive to reunite in a world fraught with danger. It's a story not just of this one biological family, but also of those they bring in along the way.

Indie authors rely on you as readers to spread the word. **Will you tell a friend or two about this book or write an online review?**

THE PALIMAR SAGA: BOOK ONE
REMNANT

When an immortal dies no one mourns but people notice

Immortals rule unquestioned. A family of smugglers gets in the way.

The shocking death of an immortal sends a master of shadows on a quest for the killer. Jon Therman and his family of sunrock smugglers stumble into this manhunt. A former slave, he only desires to live unnoticed and to avoid the corruption of the world. But when an immortal pursues his children, Jon retaliates.

His daughter, Ella, attempts to rescue her friend from a ritual sacrifice. To do so, she must defy the commands of her fellow smugglers. Jaded spy Shane zem'Arta searches for his missing commander. His orders complicate Ella's effort to save her friend and Jon's mission to protect his family, leading these old friends on a perilous adventure.

Smugglers, rogues, and lords clamber to stand against a powerful cult of immortals. Can these fragile factions set aside their mistrust to survive a burgeoning war, or will they fall divided?

Remnant, the first installment of the epic flintlock fantasy series, The Palimar Saga, introduces a world of magic, trolls, shapeshifters, and guns. Embark on this gripping gaslamp adventure filled with magic, intrigue, and battle. With a richly detailed world reminiscent of works like The Kingkiller Chronicle by Patrick Rothfuss and The Powder Mage Trilogy by Brian McClellan, *Remnant* presents a realm where immortals walk among us, and every action carries weighty consequences.

Visit palimarsaga.com to learn more.

Read the first two chapters on the following pages.

REMNANT: CHAPTER 1

DEATH OF AN IMMORTAL

The Temple of Ize, Southern Corigon
May 7, 1189 PT (Post Tyrannus)

Mavell

The stench of decay stung Collector Mavell's throat. He tightened the black scarf over his nose and mouth, stepping aside as another collector dragged a guard's petrified body by the ankles.

"Wait." Mavell's monotone voice echoed in the marble room.

The collector halted, wiping sweat off her forehead with her own scarf.

Using his bloodied boot, Mavell knocked a dart loose from behind the guard's ear. The smell of rotting fruit rose from the hollow tip—wraith poison.

Like all the fallen guards in the room, this man's rifle remained slung across his shoulder, his pistol in its holster. Fifteen armed men, but not one had fired his gun.

The scene reminded Mavell of a knacker's yard with no care given to quality butchering. This, however, was the Hall of Hoven in the Temple of Ize, a sanctuary of Drawlen. After examining the room, Mavell knew this was no haphazard slaughter. Just a gruesome work of art.

He nodded to the woman.

She grunted, heaving the stony body over the threshold. Two other collectors cleaned the remaining gore with buckets of steaming water. The distant whimpers of a child melded with the clamor of sloshing mops, boots on stone, collectors exhaling their nausea.

"Collector Mavell." His partner stepped into the room and stood at attention. Grime smattered her usually pristine uniform—an assemblage of black clothing, scarf, and belt ordered with lethal accessories. She stared with blank lavender eyes.

"Collector Detoa," Mavell said, sparing her a glance.

"He is here."

An ominous man appeared in the doorway as Detoa moved aside. He was unnaturally tall and draped in dark, silver robes, his face covered by a glittering fabric rippling like water.

Mavell dropped to one knee and bowed. Detoa and the other two collectors imitated him.

The Veiled Man stood, unmoving, for several minutes. Then he entered the room, one foot mechanically following the other. By the time his lord passed, Mavell's knee throbbed.

"Rise," came a nasally voice from under the silver veil. "Show me the body."

"Bodies, Your Eminence." Mavell gestured to the carnage. "There are twenty-three—well, almost twenty-three."

The Veiled Man regarded Mavell.

Even with the immortal's face covered, Mavell tensed under his piercing stare. "Seven of them are just heads. They were killed elsewhere and brought here as a message."

"Blood for blood." The Veiled Man pointed his gloved finger to the dais, above which the phrase SANGUINIS PRETIUM SANGUIS dripped in crimson letters. The Veiled Man's arm disappeared into his robes like a stone sinking in oil. "I have no interest in the mortals, Collector. Show me Hoven."

Mavell bowed and led the Veiled Man to the end of the hall while the other collectors resumed their work. At the other end of the space, a golden throne hid beneath a cloth, and crusted blood lined parts of the exposed metal. Mavell peeled the fabric off the upper half of the corpse entombed on the seat.

The Veiled Man stepped back. "Is that—" He pointed to a bloody mass stuffed inside the corpse's mouth.

"Hoven's heart, yes." Mavell removed the remaining cloth, displaying Hoven's erupted chest. "This was done by someone with an intimate understanding of an immortal's regenerative power."

Curling his long fingers, the Veiled Man balked.

Mavell replaced the sheet. "We have a genuine godkiller on our hands, Your Eminence."

"Indeed." The Veiled Man stretched his neck. "Why Hoven? What was the motive?"

"Vengeance, I'm sure." Mavell pointed to another covered mass in the corner while motioning to Detoa. Walking past him, she and two collectors pulled off the black fabric. It slithered to the floor, revealing the massive dragon-like head of a great-horned wyvern.

Three sets of eyes reflected the blue light of the sunrock lanterns. One of its onyx horns, curled back from the wyvern's flat nose, had been broken in half. The scales of its bruised face had withered and grown pallid. Within its gaping mouth, skewered onto its long teeth, sat seven petrified human heads. And the smell . . .

"Cover it. Burn it," the Veiled Man said. "Explain, Collector Mavell."

"According to the keeper of this temple, Hoven's clerics dispatched the wyvern to clear the way for a mining venture sixty miles east, across the border in Yvenea." Removing his knife, Mavell tapped the creature's mouth. "These seven heads are those of the clerics and a few Yvean conspirators. Other than Hoven, there were fifteen guards, an oracle, and her young daughter—all present in the room at the time of the incident."

"Why so many guards?"

"The oracle must have told him something was coming."

The Veiled Man nodded. "All were killed, I presume."

The corners of Mavell's cheeks lifted behind his scarf. "Two survived—the girl and the oracle. Although the oracle was unconscious, they were mostly unharmed."

"Bring me the girl," the Veiled Man said.

Mavell signaled to Detoa, who bowed and left the room. Standing rigidly, Mavell waited with his master. He glanced at the throne where Hoven had ruled the south with notorious cruelty for three hundred years. That immortal legacy ended abruptly, and a child was the only living witness to his death.

Detoa returned with the witness, who shuffled into the room with her neck drooping. As they approached the Veiled Man, the girl held fast to Detoa's arm.

Placing two spindly fingers under her chin, the Veiled Man raised her head. "Show me what you have seen, child." He lifted his veil. For a moment, the girl's eyes widened, their light returning. She trembled with her mouth agape. When the Veiled Man dropped his covering, the girl resumed her limp posture.

"It seems our killer is plagued by a small conscience," the Veiled Man said. "He spared the woman and her child."

"Killer?" Detoa said. "A *single* killer?"

"There was an accomplice. Both, I believe, were ralenta. But most of the killing was done by one man."

"How is that—"

"Impossible," drawled a voice from the doorway.

Mavell's teeth clenched when Selvator Kane, a dark-haired boy in an embroidered purple justaucorps and polished boots, strode into the room.

Not really a boy. Just a monster in the skin of a boy.

"How indeed, Lord of the Veil?" Sel approached, crossing his arms like a parent waiting for a child to explain his misbehavior.

The Veiled Man snorted. "Are you not the Lord of Whispers, Selvator? Did you come to be of help, or to act as your revered father's errand boy again?"

Sel bristled, but his voice remained steady. "I'm simply here for the child. Young Haana has latent shade craft, so for your sake, I hope you did not harm her."

"Indeed not," the Veiled Man said. "I have lifted the burden of this horrific event from her mind. She will henceforth have no memory of it. So, if anything, I have helped her."

Sel narrowed his eyes. "And what have you done with that—burden?"

The Veiled Man tapped his temple. "It is safe and waiting for his lordship to witness for himself."

"Then I shall take you to Lord Refsul immediately. I will meet you on the wraith gate." Sel took Haana's hand and escorted her through the door.

Once again, the Veiled Man stood, silent and still. Once again, his servants waited, just as silent, just as still. Only Haana's footsteps echoed down the stone corridor.

At last, the Veiled Man faced Mavell. "We shall speak in private, Collector."

Mavell nodded, calling his shades to cloak them. Wisps whirled like smoke from an extinguished candle, encasing them in a soundproof cocoon of darkness.

"I am giving you a secret assignment, Collector. Find this godkiller."

"Dead or alive?"

"Oh, trust me, young hunter, you and any mortal in all the Drawlen ranks are no match for this creature. He is *mortari*, a Shard Keeper, a reincarnation of Agroth. You will find him alive, and you will leave him alone."

The words *mortari* and *Agroth* swirled in Mavell's mind. They sounded familiar, but he nodded rather than risking ignorance before his master.

"You will tell no one what I show you, Collector, other than your partner. There are pieces of the child's memory only you and I will see. Not even Lord Refsul, himself, will know the nature of this adversary. Do you understand?"

"Yes, my lord."

His master put two fingers under Mavell's chin and lifted his own veil, revealing a pair of solid, white eyes. A vision of this room before the present gore flooded Mavell's mind.

He was crouched behind a pillar near the dais. No, not crouched. Beneath him, Haana's face reflected in a water basin.

Hoven, in all his obese glory, reclined on his golden throne. A red-haired woman of immense beauty, Tessa the oracle, stood rigidly at his side. Her perfection was only tarnished by the look of disgust on her face.

"You broke your word," she said.

"I am a god, Tessa. I get whatever I want, no matter what deals you try to make. You say someone is coming to kill me. I say let them try." He thrust out his sagging arm and surveyed the guards posted along the walls.

"No. You won't be getting anything you want," Tessa said.

"Why is that?" Hoven's hand snaked up Tessa's thigh, slipping under the gold fabric of her dress.

"I told you. I saw your death."

"You lie."

"A foreseer cannot lie."

The crystals in the sunrock lanterns extinguished, a shadow falling over the windows like a curtain. Muffled screams erupted while the power of a ralenta's shades momentarily blinded Haana. A minute later, fifteen dead guards lay exactly where Mavell first found them.

Tessa struggled to free her wrist from Hoven's fat-handed grip. He grunted and tossed the slender woman. Tessa's head struck the wall, and she fell unconscious and bleeding. Hoven drew a gaudy blade as he barked in horror.

In front of him sat the head of the wyvern with seven human heads skewered on its yellow fangs. Haana's eyes moved toward two hooded figures in the middle of the hall. A tall, lanky ralenta held a curved, bloody knife in each hand.

Next to him stood the godkiller. His eyes blazed behind the shadow of his hood. A long, glittering red knife protruded from his sleeve. He stepped forward with preternatural speed, then vanished. After a low, quick buzzing, he reappeared in front of Hoven. He lifted the knife and—

Haana buried her face in her arm. When Hoven's laughter filled the room, she lifted her head, eyes widening. Hoven clenched the godkiller's forearm, fending off the knife.

"So glad we're all enjoying ourselves," the accomplice said.

With overwhelming strength, the godkiller thrust the knife forward, and Hoven's cries erupted. A red glow filled the room, intensifying with Hoven's screams, followed by silence. Enveloped in darkness, Haana wept.

When Mavell resumed reality, he was lying on the floor. His shades no longer cloaked him, having lost connection with their master. Detoa's hands rested on his shoulders, but she jumped when he shook her off and glared.

As Mavell rose, his legs quaking, the Veiled Man leaned closer. "Find him. And when you do, don't let him know. Report to me and me alone."

Brushing a greasy yellow lock off his forehead with a bloody glove, Mavell bowed. The Veiled Man faced the throne. "He won't be missed." Slowly and silently, he walked out of the room.

Mavell watched until his master was out of sight, then whispered to Detoa, "That's probably true of most immortals." As they left together, they passed through the atrium garden along the mid-level balcony. Sel and Haana came into view beside a fountain on the ground floor. The collectors slipped between two planters at the edge of the balcony to listen through the power of Mavell's shade.

"I have a gift for you from your mother." Sel draped a gold chain with a pendant over the child's neck.

The girl squealed nervously as she clutched it.

"Now we shall return to Shevak," Sel said.

"Lord Sel, what about my mother?" Haana sounded rather mature for one so young, but being a Drawlen harem child often meant growing up quickly.

"The oracle will recover." The immortal tucked Haana's blond hair behind her ears. "You'll be mine someday, when you're old enough and have come into your ralenta power. Then no one will touch you. No one but me."

Detoa scoffed. Mavell pulled back his shade as Sel, the Eternal Child of Shadow, led his unsuspecting charge through the glass doors into the courtyard. The two collectors moved along the balcony for a closer view below. In the courtyard, the Veiled Man occupied the octagonal platform of the wraith gate. Sel ascended the eight steps, holding Haana's hand.

Three bronze rings rotated within the gutters upon the wraith gate and eight bronze poles rose from holes at each corner, grinding and spinning against their stone housings. Attaching to each pole like a net, a fog of shadow solidified for a second before vanishing, along with the three people. The poles sank, disappearing beneath the intricately carved platform. The bronze rings slowed to a stop.

The two collectors stared at the empty gate from the balcony. "I never thought Selvator Kane to be sentimental, or a child-lover." Wrinkling her nose, Detoa picked at a blotch of dried blood on her sleeve.

"He's neither." Mavell leaned against the railing. "He's grooming her for a convenient binding. He'll be quite disappointed when he finds out she doesn't have a shred of ralenta power. Too bad for the girl. Sel is a wolf among wolves."

"How can you know she has no shade craft when she's only five?"

He pointed to his forehead. "I've seen through her eyes. By the way, what do you recall about the name Agroth?"

Detoa stared, her brows wrinkling. "Agroth. Man or immortal?"

"You tell me."

"I think . . . hmm. Something to do with the Fires. Or maybe the Devourer."

He licked his crooked teeth. "Ah yes, the ancient terrion king who was given the power of Absolute Death by Sovereign. When he died, priests divided his power among his warriors to continue fighting the Devourer."

"They were called the Order of Mortari, weren't they?" she asked.

Mavell adjusted his scarf. "Indeed. Supposedly, Agroth reincarnated during the Fires and killed the first legion of immortals."

"Perhaps he's returned." Detoa tapped a finger against her mouth. "Perhaps he killed Hoven."

"The dead remain as they are, Detoa. But the power Agroth wielded was enough to kill countless immortals. That power may indeed live on, and it appears someone has started using it again."

REMNANT: CHAPTER 2

VULTURES

Lorinth, Taria
May 3, 1190 PT
One year later

Jon

Jon Therman's shoulders sagged under his damp wool coat. He shifted on the wagon bench, loosening the reins of his wood ox. The stout creature shook its shaggy head and trudged through the mud. Wind beating against Jon's aching back, he stood to stretch.

Sitting beside him, Shane zem'Arta slept while leaning on the brace, his boots resting on the rail. The hood of his tattered coat partially covered his face, exposing his open mouth full of pointed teeth. Water dripped from the silver-blond scruff of his neck; it trickled under his collar. Despite the cold rain, the mercenary relaxed as if basking in the sun.

Must be a troll thing. Jon smirked.

He thought of the sunrock furnace in his parlor as the fog of his breath rolled into the May air. After a month of traveling, Jon longed for his wife's warm embrace. The ghost of her laughter played upon his ears, and his fingers tingled at the memory of her silky auburn hair. Ahead of him, however, a mining caravan stretched for several miles.

Wood oxen pulled wagons loaded with sunrock. One of the animals stumbled, its belly sinking into the mud. The convoy stalled. While cursing and kicking, a worker yanked on the animal's upturned horns, only for his foot to tangle in its mane. He slipped. The creature dragged him a few steps before he rolled free.

Drawlen militiamen in tan uniforms accompanied the caravan transporting smith-grade stones. These heat-bearing rocks were worth stealing if one was daring enough.

Jon urged his wood ox over a rise, Shane jostling next to him.

The dreary town of Lorinth lay in the valley before the Deep Wood bordering Taria. As if some force held it back, the forest of tall, twisted trees arced north. A barren field stretched for a half mile between the woods and Lorinth.

The slate roofs and stone streets held a sheen with murky puddles dotting the square. Like Jon's wagon and the caravan, the black paint on the buildings peeled, evidence of a temperamental winter.

From Jon's vantage point on the west road, the southern highway stretched like a bending river across the hill-dotted landscape. Merchant carts clogged the road, fighting through muddy trenches. Only a few vendor tents populated the market square. The impending Life Harvest—the twice-per-decade Drawlen pilgrimage—usually drew a bustling business to this sleepy village.

Then he saw it. There was no mistaking the gray-clad rider galloping across the field from the north. A Drawlen ranger advanced, skirting the town and picking up speed. Jon pulled the reins of his wood ox to a mewling halt.

Shane woke, planting his feet for a pounce and placing a gloved hand on the pistol at his belt. At the same time, a crash came from within their covered wagon.

Jon swiveled at the noise.

His teenage daughter emerged, pulling open the canvas flap. "What's the deal, Papa?"

Ella's coat rested loosely over her shoulders, her curly brown hair matted and pressed to one side.

"Stay in the back, mouse," Shane said.

She glared, pursing her lips much like her mother. "Stop calling me that!"

"There's a *vulture* coming, Ella." Jon gently closed the flap.

Shane clenched his fists.

Jon nudged him. "You'd better get back there too, you know. These are Drawlen rangers. A troll in these parts will mean a lot of questions."

Shane scoffed but obliged, lifting the flap. "I thought you said your town was quiet." Then he disappeared inside the wagon.

Jon sighed as he tied the bonnet. He scratched the back of his left hand, where his open-fingered glove covered the Drawlen brand once marking him as a slave. A familiar anxiety flooded his mind: This new life was a dream. He would wake up, a slave boy in the mining barracks, chained to a wall.

His chest tightened as the rider's face came into view a few yards ahead of him. Joran Wilde returned Jon's cautious stare. The metal emblem of a hawk glinted on the sleeve of his uniform. *A lieutenant.* It had been years since Jon had seen his brother-in-law; he'd been deemed bad company for a Drawlen officer. Joran's jaw was set, his lips drawn tightly, his eyes harder than what Jon remembered. He looked like a true soldier of a Drawlen order as he sped past on his sweating brown steed.

Jon shivered.

Children's laughter cut through the moment. Jon's two sons leapt and ran along the wagon caravan toward him.

Jeb arrived first, loose russet curls bouncing over his eyes. He dove onto the bench and linked his skinny arm with his father's, whispering, "Nate got into a fight with Will Loren again."

Jon chuckled, brushing grass from the eight-year-old boy's coat.

"Jeb, you traitor!" Nate yelled.

Jeb stuck out his tongue just as Nate's foot sank into a puddle.

Nate sported a cracked lip and a purple bruise on his left cheek. His wool coat now donned as much mud as it did patches, and he skipped with a limp. Having freed his boot from the mud, he scrambled into the cart and beamed at his father. "It was a . . . friendly sorta fight."

"Did you shake his hand with your face, then?" Ella emerged from the back of the wagon and wedged herself between Jeb and Nate on the bench. She met her father's gaze and discreetly glanced at the floor of the wagon, indicating Shane had hidden himself in the smuggling compartment.

"Hey, I was defending *your* honor, ya know."

"Oh? Does my honor need defending by an eleven-year-old boy when I'm out of town?" Ella smiled and poked Nate's bruised cheek, but he swatted her hand.

Jeb giggled. "Will said he was going to give you a kiss for your fifteenth birthday, El. Nate knocked him right to the ground." He swung his fist through the air.

Ella's face flushed as she shoved her hands into the mass of her coat. She fumbled for a reply when a rustling in the grass disrupted their conversation.

A pale, sickly man broke through the sagebrush and stumbled across the road. Clad in a worn smock and metal wrist cuffs, he was sweat-soaked and bloodied. A bang echoed over the valley with the man's next step, accompanied by the thud of a round shot. Blood spattered from his chest as he collapsed into the mud.

Lieutenant Joran sat on his horse further into the field, rifle aimed and still smoking. He steered his horse to the body and began the tedious task of reloading the weapon. When finished, he slung the gun across his back and sat at attention while his horse sidestepped away from the bloody corpse, whose skin dulled and grayed with each second. Glancing briefly at Jon, Joran bowed his head and turned his eyes to the road.

Ella gasped. "Papa, isn't he—"

Jon raised a hand. "Look away, children."

Ella and Jeb stared at the floor planks, but Nate glared at his estranged uncle while another soldier on horseback trotted by and halted next to the body. Jon scowled as the man frowned at him. Captain Percy Duval was a man people went out of their way to avoid.

"Third North Rangers," Ella whispered with her head bent downward.

She really was well suited for this business.

The captain sneered at the body lying in the mud. "I would have preferred him alive, Lieutenant. This wretch had made a contract with forest demons."

Joran saluted. "My apologies, Captain. Your orders were to catch him at any cost. I aimed for his legs, of course, but the scoundrel ducked."

Jon stifled his laughter, too afraid for himself and his children. The fugitive had certainly not ducked.

Duval gritted his teeth. "Bring him to Lorinth and hang him over the temple stage. He'll get no burning. Superstition is going out of fashion, Lieutenant. We must replace it with fear."

"Yes, sir."

Duval flashed Jon a wicked grin, sending a tremor through Jon's chest. Joran steered his horse between them. "Just some bystanders, Captain."

As Duval's gaze lingered, Jon feared the ranger's schemes. He considered Shane's loaded crossbow stowed under the bench. He relaxed when the captain nodded and kicked his horse into a trot, heading toward town. Letting out a long breath, Joran dismounted next to the fallen man, now a rigid corpse.

Jon flicked the reins. The children huddled silently as the cart jostled into the ruts of the narrow highway.

Once they entered the town square, Nate jumped off the cart, skirting a puddle. "I promised Powet I'd help him in the shop today." He ran to the smithy next to Donfree's Trading Post.

Although he dodged the wheels of a passing cart, he crashed into a lamp-post. The housing shook, the door flung open, and a spray of bright, blue sun-rock powder spilled, glittering in the wind. Several identical lampposts lining the streets of Lorinth cast a haunting light against the overcast sky.

"Watch your left side." Jon waved. Before disappearing into the smithy, Nate waved back.

Jeb said goodbye and ran after his brother, leaving Jon and Ella to steer the cart around the trading post and into the barn. The boys seemed eerily unaffected by the scene they had just witnessed.

"Papa, shouldn't we shut the door?" Ella hopped off the wagon and tugged the barn door along its rusty tracks.

Jon shook himself and stepped off the cart. The door scraped along the wall as he pushed, sending flecks of black paint swirling like falling ash. When the latch clicked, Shane slipped out of hiding.

"Stay here tonight." Jon pointed to the loft.

"Abad is in town. His horses are out back," Ella said. "He could leave with you at first light."

Shane pulled his hood back, frowning. In the dim light, his eyes held their own glow, and the horizontal scars on his cheeks, one on the right and two on the left, could pass for smears of dirt. His dull, silver braid matted against his thick neck. "What about leaving tonight? I'd rather not risk a tangle with more Drawls."

"Really? I thought it was your hobby," Ella said, earning a scoff from the mercenary.

"You'd be walking *into* a tangle leaving at night with vultures in town," Jon said. "It's less suspicious to leave in the morning." He dug in his pocket and handed his daughter a coin. "Get Shane some dinner and blankets. He's going to lay low until he's *well* out of Taria."

Shane grumbled while removing his bedroll from the wagon.

Ella patted Shane on the back and left through the side door.

Jon opened the tailgate of the wagon. Removing crates and burlap sacks, he stacked them against the wall under a shuttered window. Shane shed his coat and pushed back his sleeves, revealing intricate tattoos. His leather vest still had streaks of blood from their disastrous smuggling acquisition in Estbye.

Jon moved the last crate from the wagon. "Shane?"

"Yeah, Jon?"

"Don't ever ask me to do this burning kind of work again."

"What? You're not having fun?" Shane snickered and opened the smuggling compartment. Inside lay an unconscious man—bound, gagged, and blindfolded.

"No, Shane. I'm not having fun."

Visit palimarsaga.com to learn more.

www.ingramcontent.com/pod-product-compliance
Lightning Source LLC
Chambersburg PA
CBHW070703010826
48975CB00015B/2680